BURNED TO A CRISP

A Gingerbread Hag Mystery

Book One

By K.A. Miltimore

To Mom, my earliest champion;
To Philip, my writing cheerleader;
To Lyle, my everything

Thank you.

ISBN:9781799015888

All characters and settings appearing in this work are fictitious. Any resemblance to real persons, living or dead, or to any places or locations is purely coincidental.

Cover Illustration by Bridgette Dracass

PROLOGUE

The fire licked the edges of the building and he smiled. The flames were yellow with a white-hot center, thick black smoke billowing out from the gasoline used to soak the wood. He didn't need to use gasoline but he liked the smoke it made. It would make sure the building was gone before anyone could save it, erasing any evidence, erasing everything, erasing the stain of the place itself. And gasoline was so very common. Anyone could have used it.

The heat was becoming uncomfortable. It was time for him to go, before he was seen. He wanted to linger, to watch it work, to watch the yellow fire scrub and consume and purge but his work wasn't done.

He reluctantly turned his back from the flame and saw the beady eyes of crows staring at him from the rooftop next door. The flame glinted in their black pupils. Smoke pouring out, as black as their feathers. He felt the heat on his back as he walked away. This was just the beginning.

CHAPTER ONE

It was after ten in the morning on a sunny October morning and the bakery on Griffin Avenue was still not open. That wasn't so unusual - the shop was inside the owner's home and she opened the shop when she felt like it, though not always so late in the morning. That would be peculiar for most bakers but then just about everything about Hedy Leckermaul and her bakery, the Gingerbread Hag, was peculiar. Her clients tended to be more night owls anyway, so she often kept her door unlocked until well after ten at night. In the sleepy town of Enumclaw, Washington that qualified as a night owl.

Hedy's shop was her formal parlor and large sunroom converted to a shop space. She still had plenty of room for herself, her menagerie, and the occasional traveling guest. The glass front door opened to an entry way, with a large staircase at the far end that was blocked off from customers by a beautiful wooden screen that resembled a thicket of wooden blackberry vines. To the right was the sunroom, which lead through large pocket doors into the formal parlor. Polished oak, stained glass and tufted velvet were the order of the day, but rather than stuffy, the little bakery was closer to an edible, if somewhat bizarre, curiosity shop. Hedy Leckermaul did not make common cookies or drab donuts. Hedy's treats were far stranger and definitely not to everyone's tastes.

Hedy wouldn't be ready to change the sign to "Open" on the front door until she finished her chores, and she had a late start. The cinnamon rolls shaped like walruses had risen overnight and had to be baked. The snickerdoodles with cyclops eyes were fresh out of the oven and had to be put away. She was also behind in the morning routine of the house. Hedy hurriedly made breakfast for three animals; her "menagerie" were seated around the kitchen table, impatiently waiting. It was an unlikely sight of a chinchilla, a tabby cat, and a magpie, dining on their kippers and grilled tomato breakfast. Monday was off to a late start.

With the three fed, the showcase treats stocked, and her criss cross apron placed over her plaid romper dress, Hedy switched the sign with a feeling of excitement. She had received a call from the Concierge that a traveler was coming tonight and that would bring a welcome dose of the unknown into her routine. She loved it when a traveler came to visit. The excitement of meeting someone new made all the work worthwhile.

The Gingerbread Hag was a newer shop and definitely off the beaten path, tucked away on the residential end of Griffin Avenue. It was hard to find, unless you knew it was there; nothing about the Victorian facade betrayed it was a bakery except a small sign by the curb. But those who had been there and who weren't scared away by the edible monstrosities on display came back often and brought their friends. Hedy current clientele included two knitting groups, a Girl Scout troop, a gardening club and the local chapter of the Daughters of the American Revolution. Though these customers were regulars, the strange name of the shop was a mystery to them. None of them had worked up the courage to ask.

"Good morning, Miss Hedy." The bell at the front door tinkled as her first customer of the day came into the shop. Despite the sunny day and beautiful early autumn weather, the lady had her umbrella hanging carefully from her arm.

"Good morning, Mrs. Wilson. It is a pleasure to see you today. How are the grandchildren?" Mrs. Wilson came to the shop twice a month for goodies on her way to babysit her grandchildren for the day. Their favorites were her fox tail donuts - long and taped, with shaved reddish-brown chocolate that turned to white milk chocolate on the tips. She filled them with blood red Bavarian cream so that every bite had an ooze of scarlet.

"Ah, you know they run me ragged but I love to see them. I think they would lock me out of the house if they didn't see me coming up the driveway with one of your gingerbread boxes."

Hedy placed the three fox tails into the box and tied it shut with a ribbon that looked like it was made of gumdrops. Mrs. Wilson carefully picked it up from the antique counter and handed Hedy fifteen dollars. She had never paid so much for a donut anywhere else but these were perfection.

Mrs. Wilson commented "However can you remain so trim around the constant temptation?" but Hedy only laughed, giving away no secrets.

"Thank you, Mrs. Wilson. You were smart to bring your umbrella, it is going to rain this evening." Both ladies looked toward the cloudless sky through the leaded window and nodded. Mrs. Wilson knew because her elbow hurt and her elbow always hurt before it rained. How Hedy knew was a mystery to the old lady.

The bell tinkled as she left, and the quick draft of cool autumn air ruffled Maurice's fur. He shivered. It didn't take much temperature change for him to shiver, leaving a few silky chinchilla hairs in his wake.

"I really don't see why we have to be open today, Hedy. A quiet day, catching up on my reading and sipping peppermint tea would be exactly what I would wish for." If it were possible for a chinchilla to look petulant, Maurice had the expression nailed. Hedy hardly raised her eyes from the chilled marble slab where she was rolling out pie dough.

"Maurice, there is nothing stopping you from

finishing your Proust in the peace and quiet of the library upstairs. I'd be happy to bring you some tea and your favorite beetle cookies for a snack." Maurice left the small table near the countertop where he had been perched and hopped quickly to the sideboard.

"You know perfectly well that I don't like to be alone in the library. It's a lovely room but I prefer to be down here, where it is warm and it smells like cinnamon." Maurice turned his back slightly, continuing to pout while Hedy quickly rolled the dough before it could warm up to room temperature.

"Maurice, you can say what you like about cinnamon and being chilled, but I know you don't want to go up there because of Adelaide." Hedy chuckled lightly, and though she was not in fact trying to provoke him, it had the opposite effect. Maurice turned his softball-size frame around and barely made a sound as he steamed back toward the kitchen.

"Oh Maurice, I'm sorry. I didn't mean to tease you. I know you aren't really afraid." Hedy called after him. She bit her lip slightly for lying; she knew that Maurice was indeed afraid. He feared spirits as all mammals do - all mammals save humans and cats.

Zelda, the tabby, came strolling into the room, directly in front of Maurice's path. They passed each other warily, like two old warriors who had engaged in many battles and Hedy swore she heard

Maurice mumble "harpy" as he went. To say that she and Maurice had a strained relationship would be charitable at best. Cats may not smile but Hedy saw the corners of Zelda's mouth twitch.

"I see our Maurice is having his daily hissy fit. How predictable." Zelda walked passed the counter and made her way to the patch of sun in the front of the room. The light came through the one stained glass panel, casting the shape of a spiderweb on the floor. Zelda circled herself and nestled into the shape. She watched Hedy with mild interest; the woman's impossibly high hairdo always amused Zelda, as it reminded her of a large ball of white yarn.

"I do wish you would try to get along with him. You know he is a bit temperamental, but he has a good heart." Hedy finished with the pie crust and began cutting it into circles for the small pie tins.

"A good heart to be roasted, I'm sure." Zelda licked her lips and looked toward Hedy with an unblinking blank stare.

"Alright, enough of that, please. I have quite a bit of work to do today, and we will be having a traveler tonight. The guest room needs to be aired out and I'm sure we'll need a hot meal in the oven when he gets here."

Zelda said no more but gave a dainty sniff as she settled in for her morning nap. The jingle of the door did not raise her head; any customer would have to just watch their step.

The girl came in, laden with a backpack that

looked almost as heavy as she was. Hedy guessed she was probably still in high school. She looked around the room, in obvious awe and wonder, as she set the pack down by a table in the corner. She was dressed in black and had a jagged edge bob of dark hair with heavy bangs, almost hiding her brown eyes from view.

"Good morning. Welcome to The Gingerbread Hag. What can I get for you this morning?" Hedy wiped the pie crust residue from her hands, coming around the edge of the counter. She smiled slightly as the girl gave an obvious look to Hedy's shockingly white hair with its streak of black, styled in a bouffant hairstyle. Today, she had clipped tiny jeweled spiders into its heights.

"Good morning. Coffee would be great and I don't know, something sweet to go with it?" Hedy couldn't help but chuckle as the girl finished her sentence. There were definitely a few choices for sweets.

"Well, I can do both. What kind of sweet did you have in mind? I have some lovely coffee cake, a slice of pumpkin pecan bread with chocolate-chile glaze, a foxtail donut, which are quite good, if I do say so myself, lemon curd and creme cannoli...just take a look in the case here." Hedy waived expansively at the glass case and girl took a step forward. Hedy stepped back behind the counter and pulled a delicate mint green teacup from a cupboard, placing it under the tap of a large copper urn. Steaming coffee filled the cup and she placed it on a small black tray, with a tiny pitcher of cream and a footed black dish of scarlet sugar cubes.

"Wow, ummm... how about I go with the coffee cake." The girl pulled a small coin purse out of her pocket but Hedy waived her off.

"First time visitors on a sunny October morning who also are skipping school get their first purchase for free." She smiled at the girl as she placed the cake on a mint green plate and placed it on the tray.

"That obvious, huh?" The girl smiled shyly and accepted the small tray that Hedy handed to her. She made her way back to the corner table and placed it down very carefully.

"No, I'm just good at reading between the lines. Enjoy your breakfast and let me know if you need anything else."

"Thank you, ma'am," the girl said as she picked up the tea cup.

"Please, Hedy will do just fine."

An hour or so later, the girl had long since finished her treats but was still in the corner, writing in a small black notebook. Hedy left her to her own devices as she continued working on her pies, which were now numbering 13 on the counter; she preferred to work in odd numbers. Her large oven in the kitchen would be able to accommodate them but she preferred baking them in batches in the smaller oven in the shop area; it gave the room such a delightful smell. The egg wash was applied to the last pie and they were ready to bake and become blackbird berry pies. Small bird torsos, formed from pie dough, were waiting to be baked and then glazed with a black edible varnish. Hedy would then insert them into the slit in the top of the finished pies, nestling them into the filling of dark wild blackberries. Of all the treats she made, and there were hundreds of recipes she knew by heart, making pie was her favorite.

"Ma'am...er... Hedy, could I trouble you for a glass of water?" The girl's quiet voice broke the silence.

"No trouble at all, dear, but it will cost you." The girl gave a surprised look and began to fish out her coin purse. "No, not money, information. What's your name?" Hedy brought over a large pink glass filled with crushed ice and water, placing it on the table.

"Mel," was the simple reply.

"Well, it's lovely to make your acquaintance, Mel. You are welcome here anytime. The shop hours can be somewhat erratic but we are generally open sometime in the morning until sometime before midnight, six days a week."

"Thank you. It's a beautiful place and your coffee cake was delicious. I like the quiet here, so much nicer than the library at school."

Hedy could have asked her about school, about why she wasn't there today when she ought to have been, but she didn't wish to push the girl. She would share in her own time.

"Would you like a little tour, Mel?" I can point out a few of the interesting things here on the main floor of the house. I warn you though, it might not be for the faint of heart." Hedy smiled as she spoke but she could tell that Mel wasn't sure what to make of that. Still, she seemed curious and Hedy loved showing off her collection.

"Please. I would love to see it." The girl took a quick sip of her water and rose from the table.

"Well, first off the small square stained-glass window to your left - the one that looks like a spiderweb. That is identical to the windows in the Winchester House in San Jose, California. If you don't know the Winchester House, it's rather famous as the creation of Sarah Winchester who was told she had to continuously build on the house in order to confound the ghosts of all the people killed by the Winchester rifle. I managed to procure the window panel through a rather heated game of poker a few years back. Gorgeous, isn't it?" Hedy led the girl back into the entry, and paused by a glass dome that contained a large stuffed black bird.

"You have probably heard of Edgar Allan Poe, or even studied his work in school, yes?" Mel nodded. "Well, on a trip to Baltimore many years ago, I was fortunate enough to come upon the Raven that had inspired Poe's famous work. Everyone thinks that the bird's name was Nevermore, but it was really Charlie. Alice, our resident magpie, detests this display and would like me to bury him in the backyard." Mel laughed at the thought of a magpie having concerns about a stuffed raven, but Hedy appeared to be serious. *Does this lady talk to animals*, Mel wondered.

"On a trip to Bavaria, I came upon a peddler who had a most unusual and ancient flute, with dark connotations. Have you heard the tale of the Pied Piper, who was hired by the town of Hamelin to lead away the rats? Well, the story is definitely a bit darker in truth. The town of Hamelin hired him to lure away the rats and he did that but then the town refused to pay him. His revenge was to use this flute to lure away all but three of the town's children, who were never seen again." Hedy picked up the small wooden flute and offered it to Mel to hold, who shook her head firmly.

"How do you know this is that actual flute?"Mel asked as Hedy placed it back on the small shelf before responding.

"As someone who collects curious objects, I make it my business to only deal with those that are credible and who know the cost of selling fakes." Hedy said it sweetly but there was a slight edge to her voice.

"What is that brown shingle inside that shadowbox?" Mel walked across to the dark brown box hung prominently in the center of the entry, flanked by long taper candles.

"Oh, that is my most cherished family heirloom. It has been in the Leckermaul family for over four hundred years, passed down from mother to daughter. It's why I named this shop The Gingerbread Hag." Mel turned to look quizzically at Hedy.

"Fairy tales are sometimes based in truth, even if it is just a kernel or so. Some of them have dark origins, like the Pied Piper, but some of them have been twisted and changed through the years. Such is true with Hansel and Gretel. My ancestor, Rusalia, was the witch in the story. That shingle in the frame was all that was left of her house after the villagers burned it down."

"So she was a witch? And did she really try to eat the children?" Mel felt her skin go cold at the thought. *And this woman is a baker? What on earth does she bake?*

Hedy laughed. "She may have been a witch, but she never tried to eat those kids, or at least I like to think that she didn't. As stories often do, they change over time. When the Grimms decided to write their fables, they took legend and lore and made it suit their purposes. It was a better story to make it about an evil hag who had a gingerbread house to lure children, then a story about parents who abandoned their children."

Hedy led Mel back toward the sunroom and the smell of the baking pies. She could tell by the girl's expression that she wasn't so sure she believed Hedy and that made Hedy smile to herself.

"Well, enough of dark stories on such a day. I have cookies to bake. You are welcome to look around the entry at the other curiosities. There is a gate at the end of the hall though, please don't go upstairs. That is reserved for my guests." Hedy said in a pleasant voice, resuming her work behind the counter.

"Oh, you have guests that stay here as well? Is this some kind of B&B?" Mel returned to her coffee and took a sip. *No, nothing tasted funny. She didn't want to wind up in a cage in the basement.*

"Yes, now and then I have guests who stay with me. I suppose you could call it a B&B of sorts. It's a select group of visitors, people who might be considered eccentric. I have one coming tonight as a matter of fact and I'm sure he doesn't eat children, if that is still on your mind." Hedy laughed to see the girl's face blanch. "Go on, finish your breakfast. Maybe I'll tell you the secret ingredient after you're done." Hedy laughed again and headed back to her pies.

CHAPTER TWO

As the morning became afternoon, customers came and went in a slow but steady trickle, buying pies and cookies, muffins and brownies. Hedy knew most of them. The shop had only been open since the spring and it had been a slow start to business but Hedy was fine with that. She wasn't looking for a throng of people at her door; she was happier with interesting customers rather than a crush of people, and after all, the shop was only her secondary concern.

Maurice had not returned since he stormed out earlier and she made a mental note to seek him out before the afternoon turned to evening. His nose was probably in his book and the slight, while not forgotten, was certainly not keeping him away. Zelda had finished her nap and retreated back to the kitchen, where she had re-positioned herself into a ball near the pot belly stove. Alice, the magpie, was presumably off doing magpie things because she hadn't been seen since breakfast. Mel, having finished her snacks and her head swimming with macabre German fairytales, had gathered her things and said goodbye. Hedy expected she would be seeing the young woman again in the days ahead. She hoped so, she seemed like a nice girl.

And so, the afternoon wore on, with the sun beginning to dim and the light changing closer to the evening hour. The front door bell tinkled and a stranger entered the shop.

"Are you still open, madam?" His German accent was very slight but noticeable. Under his arm, he carried a dark red satchel.

"Yes indeed. We will be open for a few more hours surely, although I do plan to close early when a guest arrives."

The man walked up to the counter, fishing in his pocket as he did so. He drew out a card with a series of circles, four stacked like a "T" and a fifth across the center - all linked and interconnected. He passed the card across the countertop.

"Oh, I guess we are closing now after all. You are early, sir. I expected you later tonight, but you are most welcome." He took the card back and put it in his pocket as Hedy came out from behind the counter and walked toward the front door. She flipped the sign to Closed and returned to the stranger.

"I hope it is not an inconvenience, madam. There is no need to close your shop on my account." The stranger was slim and tall, with neat, brownish-red hair and brown eyes, and wrapped up in a brown overcoat. He reminded Hedy of some movie version of Sherlock Holmes.

"Not at all, sir. It is no inconvenience - it is my duty and my pleasure as a waystation for travelers such as yourself. Please come in and make yourself comfortable." She waived him toward the same table where Mel had sat earlier. Hedy busied herself behind the counter, placing a fresh cookie and a cup of coffee on the small tray for her latest lodger.

"Thank you, madam. My name is Bren Aldebrand. I am very pleased to make your acquaintance." The man accepted the tray with a small smile, and paused to take a sip of his coffee, nodding appreciatively. His host was a curious figure with that shocking white hairstyle and the pale and freckled skin, yet a youthful face.

"Are you planning to be with us for a while? You've come during a lovely time of the year, with autumn colors and clear days near the mountains." Hedy brought her own cup of coffee over and sat at the table with Bren.

"I had planned to stay a week or so, if that is acceptable. I have been traveling for some time and frankly, I am a bit weary and could use the rest before I continue my journey." Bren took another sip of his coffee and settled a bit more into his chair. Hedy could see the wear of it on his face.

"We would be pleased to have you. The Concierge had mentioned you were coming, as my standard accommodations were not going to be sufficient for your...needs. I gather you have been traveling for some time; I received word quite some time ago to expect your arrival." Hedy found it strange that the traveler kept his focus on the coffee cup, rather than looking her in the eye.

"Yes, I have been on the road for ages it seems. I have been using the waystation network for months, and frankly, I am exhausted by it all." He finally looked up, and Hedy found his eyes warm if somewhat guarded. She wondered if the little wrinkles at their corners were due to his journey.

"If you like, I can show you to your room and you can rest until dinner. There will be time later to chat." Bren nodded, taking a quick sip of the coffee and bringing the cookie with him as he rose from his seat. Hedy led the way back to the entry and to the large staircase with the bramble gate blocking the way. She found the hidden latch that kept the gate in place; once unlatched it easily folded back against itself, opening the staircase.

"That's quite ingenious. The gate looks impenetrable." Hedy smiled as she led Bren up the stairs, their steps were silent on the thick Turkish carpet.

"Yes, like Rapunzel's thicket. I had to find a way to keep customers from venturing upstairs into the private part of the house. The gate looks much trickier than it really is, as is the case with most puzzles." They followed the stairs up, curving as it went to the second floor. The walls were peppered with shadowboxes and curios, and portraits with dour faces. At the second-floor landing, Hedy turned to the right and opened a large door, leading into the room for Bren.

Apart from a rather strange stone lounge, the room was a standard affair. The windows faced the east, there was an ornately carved wardrobe against the wall, and a door that no doubt led to a bathroom. Bren set his satchel on the foot of the bed.

"I hope you find everything comfortable. We'll have dinner at six if you'd like to join us then. The library is down at the end of the hall, feel free to visit it. I'll pop in there now to let Adelaide know that you are here."

"Adelaide? Another traveler is here?" He hadn't expected that.

"No, Adelaide lives in the house, or rather, she used to live here. She is a spirit and she haunts the house now. But don't worry, she isn't prone to mischief - well, not much mischief anyway." Hedy left her guest with a surprised expression as she closed the door behind her.

* * *

Dinner was a simple affair, though Hedy had used the formal dining room rather than the usual kitchen table. Meatloaf and mashed potatoes looked a bit fancier on the pale pink glass china that she liked to use for company. Bren found himself seated at the table with a cat, a chinchilla, and his hostess. Apparently, the magpie had not returned from her outing that day.

"Welcome to Bren, our guest this week. We are very glad to have you here, aren't we, Zelda and Maurice?" Hedy raised her glass of Syrah and took a sip. "Dig in, everyone. Bren, we'd love to hear about your journey, if you are inclined to share with us." She speared a few coins of carrot on her fork and swirled them in the beef gravy puddle on her plate.

"Thank you for the welcome. I am glad to be here. I've been traveling a while, only recently arriving in the region when the cargo ship from China docked in Seattle. I'm making my way east, toward New York City." If he was surprised at the introduction to the animals or that they were eating at the table, he didn't say so.

"That's certainly a long journey, from China to New York. I can't imagine how long the whole thing would take." Hedy took another sip of her wine.

"Why not simply catch a plane to New York? What with modern air travel being what it is." Maurice spoke up for the first time since that morning. He didn't worry about the traveler's reaction to a talking chinchilla; if someone was staying with Hedy, they themselves were likely stranger than himself and anyway, Maurice rarely worried about the niceties. With age came certain luxuries.

Bren only paused a moment, which was a credit to his composure, and Hedy felt terribly guilty for not properly preparing him for the situation. It had been awhile since she had dined with anyone other than the menagerie and she forgot that their speech wasn't expected.

"That is a fair question, Maurice. I would like to travel by air but unfortunately, I cannot do so. I'm rather combustible, and the change in pressure for flight would be more than I could contain. Perhaps you will permit me to ask the question as to how I can understand you. I hope you don't find the question rude." Maurice had his mouth open to reply when Zelda interrupted.

"Combustible, you say?" Zelda appeared for all the world to arch what would be eyebrows on a human face.

"Yes, Zelda. Bren is one of the four elementals, a member of the salamander clan. He is our first such guest. Remember when we had the stone lounge installed? It was for him." Zelda did not seem mollified by that answer.

"Salamanders are fire beings. The only reason I appear in this human form right now is that I am controlling my appearance through my will. This control takes energy and effort. I can do so for quite a while but eventually, I must take my fire form for a rest." The strangeness of explaining the essence of salamanders to a cat was not lost on him.

"So, your human form is just a trick then?" The cat sounded suspicious.

"No, it isn't a trick. I am a human in that I need to eat, breathe and sleep, as all humans do. But I also contain fire, fire which grows with intensity and power as I age, until it will reach a point where I can no longer control it and I become fire. Salamanders do not reach old age in their human form. They become fire fully, or they are extinguished. But that is why I am on my journey - to find a release from my fire."

It was Hedy's turn to be surprised. She had never heard of an elemental seeking to be released from their form. "Is such a thing possible?"

"There are those who say so, though I have yet to find real proof. Stories led me to the mountains of China, where I consulted with a mountain sage who told me that the only person she knew who had ever released a salamander lived now in New York City. I am on my way to find him."

"Well, we certainly wish you success and safety on your journey. I hope when you reach New York you will send us a postcard so we know of your safe arrival." Bren smiled awkwardly and nodded. It had been a long time since anyone cared whether he was safe or not. He wasn't sure if he liked the feeling; he preferred to be on his own as it was easier that way.

"There is smoke around you, salamander. Smoke that hides your truth." The words came from the stillness in the room and Maurice scurried down from his plate, disappearing beneath the table.

"Adelaide, please do be kind to our guest. If you care to join us, we ask you to appear, not to lurk about." Hedy gave an apologetic smile to Bren. "Please forgive Adelaide, she tends to be a bit melodramatic. She has been in the house for almost a hundred years and much of that time has been spent haunting the living who did not understand her. She has a penchant for talking in riddles."

"It's quite alright. I would say that she is most perceptive to my nature. Adelaide, I look forward to meeting your properly." Bren spoke into the room but there was no further response.

"She'll come around in her own time. Anyone care for dessert? I have an apple pie warm from the oven. I still owe you an answer about the menagerie, don't I?" Zelda and Bren were ready for the pie but Maurice had already left the room; he still wasn't comfortable around Adelaide.

* * *

Dinner was finished and Bren had insisted on helping with the washing up, though he preferred drying the dishes to submerging his hands in water. "It's not that I can't get wet, it is just that I find it rather unpleasant," he said.

"Oh, then you would not care for winters in Enumclaw, or really anywhere near here. It rains quite a bit here, as I'm sure you've heard. The Pacific Northwest is rather famous for its rain, though it isn't quite as bad as everyone says." Hedy passed the wet plates to him and he handled them quickly with the towel, stacking them on the slightly warm stovetop.

"Yes, so I have heard. I expect to be well gone from this region by the time the rains begin in earnest. But if my journey is successful, I will come back and dance in the rain and drench myself from my head to my toes."

Hedy chuckled as she imagined a former salamander dancing for joy in her yard. "I hope to see that, Bren."

"If I might ask you about being a host, I know a bit of the story of the waystations. They have been around since the early 20th century as a way for those with special abilities to be able to safely travel, correct?" Hedy nodded, though she herself only knew a bit more as to their origins.

"How did you become a host?" As far as he could tell, Hedy was just an ordinary, if somewhat bizarrely attired, woman. It seemed a strange profession for her.

"Oh, that is a bit of a long story, but I came into the network several years ago. Signing on to be a new host requires living in an established waystation for a year, as well as having the financial means to support a house. As you know, waystations are dotted across not only America but all over the world. I served my residency in a house in New Orleans, though in the case of New Orleans there was hardly a need for it in that supernatural friendly city. Have you ever been there?" Hedy pulled the plug from the drain and the dirty water began to swirl from the sink.

Bren shook his head, "No, but perhaps one day, maybe I will go there to celebrate if I am successful on this quest."

"It's a perfect town for that. Everyone should see it once. There is no place quite like New Orleans, though it can be quite dangerous, especially for those who live on the edges of regular society. As I found out first hand." Hedy chuckled lightly, but it had taken her years to remember those days without fear.

"Maybe you can be my guide then. We can be *touristischen* together, *frauline*." Bren gave her a crisp bow and took the last clean dish from her to dry. She did her best to curtsy back.

It was nearing eight o'clock but she could tell that Bren was ready to retire. "Thank you for the help with the dishes. I am a night owl, Bren, so don't mind me. I may open the shop back up in case any customers are in need of a late-night treat. Feel free to head upstairs if you wish. I hope the stone lounge works for you - you can imagine how popular I was with the local moving company. If there is something else that would be better though, please let me know."

"No, stone is perfect. I can truly rest on something that I do not need to worry about catching fire. Thank you for a lovely meal and your charming company. I do hope to meet Adelaide properly tomorrow."

Bren withdrew from the kitchen and his words

reminded her to seek out the resident spirit in the library. Ghost or no ghost, manners were still a thing of consequence in Hedy's house. She made her way up the stairs, bringing a lit candle with her, as Adelaide preferred no electric lights in the library. Hedy made her way into the dark room and placed the candle on the small table near the door. She took a few tapers from their sconces and lit them as well, bringing shadowy light to the room. The room had the faint odor of lavender and cedar, like a sachet from a grandmother's underwear drawer.

"Adelaide, I'd like to speak with you. Will you show yourself?" She waited a few moments before she saw the curtain near the window rustle and move and the form of Adelaide appear before her. The ghost was barely five feet tall and the palest of blue from the outline of her bobbed hair to the toes of her t-strap shoes. She shimmered slightly in the candlelight. The lavender scent filled Hedy's nostrils.

"I am surprised that I have to say this to you, since you have existed for as many years as you have, but your comment in the dining room was rather rude, you know. Bren is a guest in this house." Adelaide said nothing and Hedy waited for what seemed like a long time before continuing. "I know we have only lived together a short time and we've only had a few travelers these last months, but I thought we had both learned to accept and appreciate the differences in our guests and each other. I hope you will show a little effort tomorrow to be kind to him." Adelaide turned away from Hedy though she did not disappear.

"He hides a secret graver than what he shared. There is smoke around him, it hides the truth." Before Hedy could answer, Adelaide was gone, leaving the curtain rustling by the window.

CHAPTER THREE

It was another sunny and crisp autumn day, with blue sky and spectacular gold and orange leaves sprinkling the ground all along Griffin Avenue. Hedy was up a bit earlier than usual, just in case Bren was an early riser himself, and she saw the sun come up from the east porch. The sun glinting off of the glaciers of Mt. Rainier was always a breathtaking sight and one she never tired of. She ruminated over her coffee on Adelaide's words and wondered what the spirit might have meant. It wasn't the first time a traveler of dubious character had stayed with Hedy. Before moving to Enumclaw, Hedy's house in Portland, Oregon had played host to a particularly surly lycanthrope and she could only imagine what he was like during a full moon. As a waystation host, you had to expect that some of the guests would be more challenging than others. There were times when there might even be danger if the guest had tendencies that couldn't be controlled, but the number one creed for the waystation was Do No Harm to Others.

So why had Adelaide warned her about Bren? Adelaide, unlike the menagerie, hadn't been in a waystation very long - she was tied to the house, not to Hedy. Perhaps her limited experience had made her extra cautious. Despite having died in 1922, Adelaide had only been nineteen at the time of her death and her experience as a ghost had been limited to the residents of the house. If Adelaide would be willing to appear, and that wasn't always the case, Hedy wanted to see if she could learn more about her concerns. She didn't want to discount whatever was making Adelaide uneasy but it might just be a case of not understanding the nature of their guest.

Empty coffee cup in hand, she smoothed out her apron and set to work to make her fresh glazed cinnamon snail rolls.

The bell tinkled when the first customer came in an hour or so later; She had left two cinnamon snails and a carafe of coffee on the table outside Bren's room, but still no sign of the salamander.

"Glad to see you are open." It was Mel, clearly skipping school again.

"It's good to see you again, Mel. But I must ask, shouldn't you be in school?" Normally, Hedy didn't like to pry but two days of truancy really was something to comment on.

"Uh, well, yes and no. I am slated for early graduation and I am all caught up on coursework. The teacher just sends me to the library to hang out for the day, so I'm not missing anything. I am done with high school after this semester and I start the University of Washington in the spring." Mel seemed almost embarrassed to share that she was well ahead of her peers in academics. Hedy poured a cup of coffee and placed it on the table in the corner.

"Well, I had no idea you were a genius when you came in yesterday. I like to keep acquaintance with smart people so when a problem comes up, I might just ask you for help."

"Thanks, but I'm not really that smart. I'm just good at math - always have been. Numbers make sense to me and I like the way if you follow a formula properly, you get a consistent result."

"Kind of like baking, in that way. Though I would say the recipe is just the beginning - the real fun comes in the creativity and the bending of the rules. Speaking of that, would you care for a warm cinnamon snail? They are right out of the oven."

The morning wore on and Mel was engrossed in a calculus book, reading apparently for pleasure. A few more customers had come in, but by and large the shop was quiet. Zelda had wandered in and out and Alice, finally making her appearance, had hopped in quietly and then landed on her perch in the entry. Mel had not seemed to notice either arrival.

The bell tinkled again and two women came in, dressed in very fashionable yoga outfits and fleecy boots. From their perfect looking hair, Hedy would guess they were on their way to yoga class, not from it, though maybe they weren't heading to yoga at all.

"I couldn't believe it when I heard from Wendy this morning. The whole studio, just gone, and they haven't found Shannon yet. Do you have non-fat cappuccino?" The last sentence was directed at Hedy, who shook her head.

"Brewed coffee, I'm afraid - no espresso." Hedy watched the woman's shaped brows furrow slightly.

"Hmm. What about chai? Any chai tea?"

"Again, sorry - I have Earl Grey, Darjeeling, jasmine or chamomile teas." Again, the perfect brows furrowed, marring her unnaturally smooth forehead ever so slightly.

"Coffee with a splash of cream will work." The woman sighed dramatically before continuing her conversation with her friend.

"Seems it caught fire some time before midnight." Hedy could hear the gossipy excitement in the woman's voice, though she seemed to be trying hard to sound concerned.

"I wonder if the heating system caused it? Shannon had only installed the hot yoga space a month or so ago. I'll take the same coffee, to go, thanks." The other customer hadn't turned to face Hedy as she also placed her order, but instead was fishing out some cash from a hidden pocket in her shiny yoga pants. Sanskrit letters scrolled down her legs.

"I got it, Heather," she waived her Visa card toward Hedy before continuing, "I'd be surprised if it was the heating system. Honestly, if I had to guess, I would guess someone set it deliberately. Wendy said that the fire burned so fast that the firemen couldn't save the building. It was like gas was on it." Both women took their paper coffee cups and headed back toward the front door, muttering "thank you" as they went. With another tinkle of the bell, they were gone.

"Mel, did you hear them mentioning a fire? Did you notice anything when you were walking here?" Hedy had caught Mel's eye peeking over the edge of her book as the women were speaking.

"Yeah, I couldn't help but hear them. My house isn't near the main part of town so I didn't see anything but I did smell smoke in the air. I thought someone might be burning trash. I'm gonna look it up on my phone though." She paused for a minute and a few swipes later, she held up her phone for Hedy to see. There was a small image of a blazing fire visible across the shop. "The news says the cause of the fire is still not known but it might have been purposefully set. The owner, Shannon Williams, has not been located yet."

"Which studio was it?" Hedy had lived in town for almost a year but there were many stores and shops that she still didn't know. She hadn't done much to explore her new town.

"The one off Pioneer - not too far from the sandwich place. Luckily, it was a standalone building and not attached to anything. A whole block could have gone up otherwise."

"What an awful thing - I hope the owner is alright." Hedy gave a slight shake of her head as she spoke, as if that would chase away any danger.

"Me too. It was a popular studio, always busy and with the new hot yoga, even more people were going. Personally, I don't see the appeal of sweating in a hundred-degree room but that is just me." Mel had never found yoga very appealing. She liked track and field, especially long distance running. That made much more sense than trying to bend herself into a sweaty pretzel.

"I agree, it wouldn't be my cup of tea, but to each their own. Whatever caused it, I hope they find out soon and I hope they find the missing woman." Hedy returned her focus to the mixing bowl and Mel went back to her calculus.

The day continued with more customers coming in, with a few mentioning the fire, but generally keeping their focus on cookies and pies. The flow was steady and it kept Hedy from making any real headway on her plans for candy jack o'lanterns. She was planning to test some modeling caramel but she needed time and quiet, and the customers were just a little too steady for that to happen.

She looked up when the bell tinkled and saw her neighbor, Mr. Jeffries, entering the shop. "Good morning, neighbor," Hedy said as he approached the counter.

"Good morning. I noticed your yard is looking unkempt again. I thought you had planned to hire a gardener to keep things up to the neighborhood standards. This is a historic home, as you know. It is on the National Registry and it must be kept in top condition, including the yard." Mr. Jeffries looked at her impatiently, irritation clearly marked in the crows' feet around his small eyes. His skin was an unsightly mottled red that blended up to the faded red hair left on his head.

"Indeed, I did say that. I have not found someone willing to take on the job. Perhaps you know someone who would be interested?" Hedy could have been irritated by the man, but she refused to let his attitude ruin an otherwise lovely day.

"Your yard is your responsibility, not mine to arrange. I believe I saw a flyer up at the Safeway for a local gardener; you could start there. With autumn upon us, all the leaves are going to create quite a mess if you don't keep up on it." Hedy noticed the deep frown lines around his mouth, no doubt from too many years lacking smiles. *How did someone live that way*, she wondered.

"Thank you for stopping by to share your concerns. I will continue to look for someone." She could tell he wasn't pleased with that answer as the red in his face started creeping down his neck.

"I'll be happy to lend a hand by raking the yard today. I have time." Bren had entered the room from the entry and Mr. Jeffries turned at the sound of his voice.

"I didn't know Miss Leckermaul had anyone else staying here." Mr. Jeffries puckered his lips as he spoke. Hedy could tell he was making an assumption about Bren's presence but she did not feel inclined to correct him. Her business was none of his.

"Thank you, Bren. There is rake in the garage but you certainly don't need to feel obliged to do so. It is, after all, just leaves." Mr. Jeffries gave her sharp look before turning toward the door. "Goodbye, neighbor," she called out as he shut the door with a hard slam.

"He's charming." Bren smiled slightly as he joined her in the shop.

"Yes, Mr. Jeffries has been a delight since we moved in. There is always this faint odor of displeasure around him, like sour milk. The man hasn't even eaten a cookie, which tells me right off the bat he is not to be trusted. I try not to judge a book by its cover, but his cover makes me think of mildew." Hedy smiled and she heard Mel chuckle from behind her book in the corner.

"Well, I'll go rake the leaves and perhaps that will appease him for now." Bren left the room and the ladies heard the front door bell tinkle.

"I've never seen him before. Is he new in town?" Mel inquired almost immediately.

"Oh, that was rude of me, I should have introduced you. He's that visitor I mentioned and he's just passing through. He's only staying with us a few days, that's all." Hedy could feel Mel's eyes on her, though she hadn't looked up.

"Too bad he won't be staying longer. The town

can always use more interesting people. He reminds me of an actor I've seen, tall and kinda good looking. Like that guy that played a detective, Cumbersomething...He's cute, right?" Hedy looked up briefly to catch Mel smiling at her before resuming her book.

Hedy made a disapproving shushing sound but she did wander over to the window to watch Bren bring the rake out of the garage. Maybe he was a little handsome, but that wasn't important. He was a guest and besides, Hedy remembered all too well what happened when she got involved with a guest, back in New Orleans.

"Sherlock Holmes. You are thinking of Sherlock Holmes, Mel. That's who he looks like." Hedy watched the girl barely look above the edge of the book, but she could tell she was smiling behind the pages.

"Looks like Dr. Strange to me. He's the one you said didn't eat children, right?" Mel chuckled, no doubt remembering Hedy's story from yesterday.

"Well, as far as I know he doesn't eat them. He hasn't made any special requests for dinner. If he does though, you'll be the first one I come to." Hedy gave Mel a look that could have meant Mel would be on the menu.

"I suspect I wouldn't be very tasty, so I'd stick with chicken. Everything tastes like chicken, right?" They both laughed at that. Hedy had never hosted a cannibal; she definitely would draw the line there.

"Whatever dark secrets he has, I doubt he'll be here long enough for us to learn them. Best to get back to our own business, huh?" Hedy gave Mel a nod and they both returned to their work, the news of the fire forgotten.

CHAPTER FOUR

Normally, Hedy tried to get all her grocery shopping done for the week on Sundays when the shop was closed, but today she found herself in need of a few staples and she decided to run out for quick trip during the day. Mel had left, so Hedy switched the sign to "Closed" and headed down the stairs toward her car. She'd remembered to take off her apron, which was a good start and not always a given. Her dress was a purple sleeveless shift and she had tossed on an orange cardigan against the breeze, the color reminiscent of her freckles. Her hair was more bouffant than beehive today and with the amount of AquaNet she used, it would survive more than any passing wind; Enumclaw was notorious for strong winds.

The town had a main grocery store, a specialty meat market a seasonal farm stand and plenty of backyard farmers who sold eggs and honey. Today, Hedy just needed some butter and few essentials for dinner so she headed over to the local Safeway. It happened to also be near the site of the fire and she was curious to see what remained of the building.

She drove slowly through town - it was the kind of town where the police kept a sharp eye for speeders. The Corvair coupe in atomic blue was not exactly a low-profile vehicle, so Hedy took care to mind the limits. Right before the Safeway parking lot, she saw the remains of the yoga studio. Blackened, charred remains were soaked with water, with shards of glass spiking the ground around it. The building hadn't been that large and the fire consumed it all, leaving only a few stubs of 2x4 framing and a few fragments of wall. She continued passed the spot and pulled into the parking lot for the store.

Inside, she noticed the bulletin board with signs for services and local clubs. Chuckling, she tore off one of the tags from the flyer for a gardener. *Maybe this would keep Jeffries off her back,* she thought. *Probably not.*

It didn't take her long to get the few items in her cart and head for the checkout stand. As someone who made everything herself, she didn't need to spend time considering frozen entrees, canned soups, or toaster tarts. Essentials were easy to shop for.

When it was Hedy's turn at the conveyor belt, she took out the three gallons of milk, four dozen eggs and six pounds of butter from her cart. For dinner, she had picked up a fillet of wild, if previously frozen, sockeye salmon. She'd bake it with some lemon and a bit of dill from the herb pots on her windowsill.

"Doing some baking?" The clerk began to scan Hedy's items, eyeing the large quantity of butter.

"You could say that. I have the bakery on Griffin Avenue. Just picking up a few items."

"Oh right, that shop in the old house. I've never been but I've heard you have... interesting things." The way the clerk's voice trailed off when she said "interesting" made Hedy think of other word choices, like "weird" or "strange".

"You should come visit and have a cookie on the house." She smiled as she started loading the milk back into her cart.

"Thank you. I might just do that." The clerk's voice didn't leave Hedy feeling hopeful. Both she and the shop weren't everyone kind of cookie and she was alright with that.

"Have you heard any news about the yoga studio fire? Did they find the owner?" Hedy wasn't one to gossip but she had a bad feeling about the situation and she wondered if there was anything new that was known.

"No, and it is so sad. The firefighters and the police have been there all morning. They searched the building top to bottom but no remains and no sign of her. They do know it was arson, but beyond that, no clues on what happened to Shannon." The clerk handed her the last bag.

"I'm so sorry to hear that. I hope they find her soon. Her family must be so worried." Hedy took her receipt, calling out as she left, "I really do hope you come by for a cookie."

Back at home and unloading her groceries, Zelda met her at the porch. Even if Zelda were capable of carrying groceries, it wouldn't be in her nature to do so. She only came to share information, and often not even that.

"You had a call while you were out." Zelda said. Hedy, unlike most of the world, still had a landline telephone and an answering machine with mini tapes. "Another traveler is due to arrive, likely tonight. Details are on the machine." Message delivered, Zelda turned and headed for the sunny corner of the porch.

"That's odd, usually we don't have much overlap. Thank you for the message, Zelda." Hedy pondered the complexities of having two guests as she loaded the groceries into the kitchen. Unlike typical guests, having two travelers at once could be more of a problem, depending on the unique circumstances of each. She'd have to listen to the message to see what she was getting into.

"Well, we shall make do as we always do, right Maurice?" Maurice was enjoying a snack of basil and buffalo mozzarella at the kitchen table.

"I suppose we shall, though why we serve host to these creatures, I don't understand. Isn't it enough that you have people coming in and out of our home all day in the shop? Must we also open ourselves up to risk with these travelers?"

"I'm surprised at you, Maurice. When did you become so uncharitable? You came into our lives when you and that dreadful traveler, Dr. Zee were in need of help in Portland. He moved on but you opted to stay. What if I had turned you away in your hour of need?" Hedy frowned at him as she stacked the butter in the refrigerator.

Maurice shuddered at the memory of the necromancer. "Point well taken. But things are different now. Times are more uncertain, more dangerous. The travelers of the past are not the travelers of today. I doubt they are all seeking refuge or protection as they were in the past - what about those who would do us harm?"

Hedy came and sat down at the table with Maurice. She thought for a moment before she answered him. "I understand the fear. But I also know that to turn away those in need, to refuse to help just because of our fear is not an option if we want to live in the kind of world we are trying to protect. Turning our backs on others not only hurts them, it hurts us. I'm not willing to do that, are you?" She reached out and gave Maurice a small tickle under his ear. "We are all too good for that, Maurice. Even Zelda." The chinchilla chortled and a bubble of spit hit his lip before he returned to his snack.

If a traveler was on the way, even if there were risks to opening her doors, she would be ready. She'd have to let Bren know though. He seemed like someone who wouldn't mind the company. The wiggle of doubt that had crept into her brain after seeing the remnants of the yoga studio popped up again. *What if the fire was caused by*

Bren? She felt guilty immediately even thinking that but an arson had just happened as a salamander came to town. *Wasn't it natural to have such a thought?*

She felt like a hypocrite. Here she was telling Maurice that fear isn't the way and she was doubting someone who by all evidence was a nice person, just because of his connection to fire. Even with the internal lecture, she couldn't stop that wiggle in the back of her brain that didn't believe in coincidence.

Hedy felt the stab of guilt again when she saw what a splendid job Bren had done raking the leaves. The yard looked magnificent. She wondered briefly why the large tree near the house seemed filled with crows, but perhaps it was a nesting tree for them.

Hedy rewarded Bren for all his help with a slice of German chocolate cake.

"Made with actual German? What would my Oma say?" he joked as she brought him a slice out on the porch. "Given your penchant for unusual foods, I wouldn't be surprised, though of course, you know this isn't a real German food, yes?"

"Ah, so amusing Mr. Aldebrand. I'll forgive the suggestion that I would use such an ingredient in my treats. Though high marks for the attempt at a joke. And yes, I know it isn't a real German treat. It's still good though, right?" She sat down next to him and gazed out at the lawn now free of maple leaves. "Mr. Jeffries should be impressed by your efforts, at least for the moment. Thank you again for offering to help."

"My pleasure. It's been a long time since I did anything as simple and comforting as raking leaves. I'll keep an eye on them while I am here to keep your neighbor off your back."

"I appreciate that. Ever since we moved in, Mr. Jeffries has managed to find something that he doesn't like and he never fails to let me know. Even so, he seems much more irritable than usual. Perhaps it is the change of the season."

"Perhaps he can't stand to see someone living their life in their own way, doing what they love. Some people have a need to squash that whenever they see it in others." Bren was savoring the mundane joy of eating a slice of cake and looking at piles of leaves. How anyone could fail to be happy at that he didn't understand.

"Well, whatever his reasons, I'll be glad to have him with one less complaint on his list. I heard today that we will be having another traveler with us, likely tonight. I hope you don't mind. It isn't usual for this waystation since we are off the beaten path, but we do have the room."

"No complaints from me. I'd welcome meeting another traveler. There haven't been that many that I have come upon as I've made my journey. I'm always open to hearing another interesting story over a delicious dinner." He took another bite of the cake. Hedy was a tremendous baker, he had to give her that.

As if on cue, a small figure with long, dark hair came into view, walking in front of the house and pausing as she checked the address. She turned and came up the long walkway, carrying two tote bags that may have weighed more than she did. The wind was blowing her hair around her in dark undulations.

"I think she has arrived." Hedy rose and came to the top of the steps to greet her. "Good afternoon, I'm Hedy Leckermaul. Welcome to The Gingerbread Hag."

"Hello. I think you may be expecting me? I have my station card in my pocket somewhere." The girl's voice was soft and hesitant as she looked up the stairs toward Hedy. She looked all the smaller with that cascade of dark hair down her back.

"You can present the card when your hands aren't full, though I'm not very good at following Concierge protocol. We are glad to have you with us. Please let me help you with your bags." Hedy came down and met the traveler mid-way, taking one of the tote bags from her.

"May I introduce Bren Aldebrand, another guest this week." Bren stood up and gave the girl a small bow. She returned the greeting and followed Hedy toward the front door.

"Thank you for your hospitality on such short notice. My name is Anahita Sohrab." Hedy opened the front door and she gave the girl a moment to let her eyes adjust from the bright sunshine to the darker space.

"Well, you are very welcome, Anahita. That is a lovely name. Persian, isn't it?" The girl nodded and Hedy led her back toward the stairs. "Let's get you settled. I have a lovely room on the second floor, adjacent to the library. I hope you will find it comfortable."

* * *

The newest guest made her way into the shop a short while later, shyly hanging back while Hedy rang up the customers who were purchasing coconut hedgehog rolls and iced cobra cookies. The customers exited the shop and Anahita came into room, admiring the display case with obvious awe.

"Did you make all these?" She seemed struck by the sheer variety of sugary treats available.

"I did indeed. I come from a long line of bakers and most of these are old family recipes. Would you care to try something?" Hedy always enjoyed seeing the look of wonder when people admired the showcase.

"Thank you, but I would rather wait until after dinner, if that is alright with you. Sweets have a tendency to spoil my appetite. But if I could trouble you for some tea, that would be most welcome." Anahita's voice reminded Hedy of water on tiny pebbles.

The front door bell tinkled; Bren was coming back into the house from his lengthy stay on the front porch. He was carrying the empty cake plate.

"Bren, would you care for some tea, or perhaps something a bit stronger?" Hedy thought his face looked a bit flushed. Perhaps the wind was colder out there than she thought.

"You read my mind, Hedy. A nip of whiskey would be just the thing, if you have it." Bren came into the shop and took a seat at the table nearest Anahita.

"What kind of a host would I be if I didn't? I'll go get it from the dining room." Hedy left the teapot on Anahita's table before bustling out to fetch the bottle.

The two travelers sat in silence for a moment before Anahita broke the quiet. "Have you been here long?" She poured the tea carefully into the cup, more to have something to do than anything else. Small talk was not her strong suit and she wasn't comfortable talking with strangers.

"No, not at all. I just arrived yesterday. I came from Seattle and I am making my way east."

"Oh Seattle, yes, I myself came up from Portland, but I am hoping to visit Seattle on my way north. In fact, I was due to stay at a waystation in Seattle but the host had a fire and was unable to accommodate me. That is why I am here. Perhaps you stayed there?" Anahita took a small sip of the tea, looking expectantly at him over the rim.

"No, I don't know anything about the Seattle waystation, I don't keep tabs on things happening in the network." Bren's voice sounded almost brusque.

Hedy returned with a crystal bottle with deep amber liquid. "On the rocks, Bren?"

"Neat, please. I'm not a fan of ice." She poured and he accepted the glass, taking a sip and nodding appreciatively. "I've never been a fan of spirits, myself. I don't like the feeling of fire in my throat." Anahita said.

"Well, fire is something I am used to, being a salamander." Bren took another sip of his whiskey and smiled at the girl. "If we are going to be staying in the same house for a few days, we might as well get to know each other, no?"

"Yes, I suppose so. Forgive me if I seem a bit awkward, but I'm not accustomed to talking about myself, especially with someone I have just met. I have never met a salamander before. We are about as opposite as two can be. I am an undine."

The surprise registered immediately on Bren's face. Almost no one had met an undine - they were exceptionally rare, even for elementals.

"It is my pleasure to meet you, Anahita. To say that we are opposites in nature would be an understatement but where else but a waystation could two such individuals ever meet." He raised his glass to toast her and she did the same with her teacup. Fire and water sitting together in a sweet shop, the most unlikely of pairs.

"And it is my pleasure to host you both." Hedy smiled at her guests and marveled at how small the world truly was. She hoped that fire and water wouldn't clash under the same roof.

CHAPTER FIVE

Wednesday dawned, again crystal clear and sunny, as early autumn often did in the northwest. The soggy days of November seemed a distant threat and the beautiful weather had inspired Hedy to create some new delights. Her large maple leaf sugar cookies were almost ready to hand paint with sheer watercolor frosting of reds and oranges, and for those who liked something a bit more sinister for their autumn treat baskets, she was working on some rather realistic look eyeball donuts.

Anahita, herself an early riser, was up with the sun and Hedy barely beat her to the kitchen. Without a word, she dove into the bowls and cookie sheets in need of a scrubbing from the morning baking.

"You are a guest, Anahita. No need to concern yourself with dishes. Please have a seat with the menagerie and keep me company."

"My mother would be appalled if I did such a thing. How quickly will we be done with this when we work together, and then we can share some coffee together. I want to hear the story of how Zelda and Maurice came to your home."

"It's a deal. We'll eat some pomegranate coffee cake and drink fresh coffee and I'll tell the tale of the menagerie. Perhaps even Bren will join us." Hedy finished the last flourish on the leaves, the royal icing serving as her palette.

"I wouldn't count on that. He was out late last night, I heard him come back not very long ago." Anahita spoke softly as Hedy finished the last bowl and wiped it dry with the red trimmed towel hanging by the potbelly stove.

"He did? I didn't hear him leave." Of course, with her room on the third floor, it was unlikely Hedy would hear anything short of a murder downstairs.

"It's true, he went out around 10:30 or so and he didn't return until almost four this morning. Quite the night owl, one might say, or phoenix in his case, given his flammable nature." Zelda piped up with the satisfaction of someone who had just cracked a witty joke. She gave her paw one more lick to be sure it was just right. Anahita took a sharp gasp of breath, exhaling it as a small stifled scream.

"Oh, how rude of me. I should have mentioned that the menagerie has the power of speech. Well, I should clarify. All animals have the power of speech but the menagerie is able to speak in English."

"But how? I've never heard of such a thing, not even in our ancient shrines at home. Surely

I would have known." She looked from Hedy to Zelda in disbelief and suspicion. She was clearly wondering if this house had some kind of magic charm about it, some evil spell that caused the animals to speak. Anahita instinctively grasped the small vial of water she wore on a filigree chain around her neck.

"No, I promise you, there is nothing malevolent or unnatural here," Hedy spoke as if reading the young girl's mind. "Truly, the only reason we can understand them is because of one of the artifacts in the entry. Come on, I'll show you." Hedy led the way toward the entry, with Anahita following warily and at a slight distance behind her.

About half way from the stairs, a long staff hung from a velvet wrapped hanger. The staff was some kind of wood, blond and finely grained. The top of the staff had two sheaves of wheat, carved as intertwined. Hedy stopped and pointed toward the staff.

"This staff is the source of our understanding. It is called Circe's staff." Anahita took a step closer to look at the lovely but rather ordinary looking staff.

"Circe? As in goddess of the harvest, Circe? Are you serious?" Anahita shook her head in disbelief, which when Hedy considered that a water spirit was the one who had no faith in such a thing, she found that quite amusing.

"It is only called Circe's staff, I have no way of knowing if the name is accurate in any way. Circe had the power to transform enemies into animals, so the legend says, with the power of her herbs and her staff. So, it would seem that the staff has the power to transform animals into friends - or at least to provide them with the power to speak so that we might understand them. I have had the staff in my possession for the last seven years and I assure you that none of my animals could ever speak until I came to own the staff."

Anahita said nothing but looked again at the staff and then back again at Hedy. She paused a few moments and then turned fully toward the woman before her.

"Alright, who are you? I wouldn't normally ask a host such a question but are you yourself a traveler? What explains this house, all these objects that you collect?" Hedy led the way back toward the kitchen and poured out the coffee before answering.

"Anahita, I am just a woman. Eccentric perhaps, certainly a collector of the strange or bizarre, but just a woman like any other. Believe me, if I had special powers, I would be working on slowing down time. I'm not a fan of aging." Hedy chuckled but her guest said nothing.

"I suppose my gift, if I have one, is that I see the world around me with clearer eyes and I accept those who are not like me. Perhaps it is the blood of my ancestor that gives me my willingness to see beyond what others see. It's not something that I worry about. I accept it as it is. You want some cake?" Anahita shook her head but accepted the coffee and sat back at the table with Zelda.

"I'm sure you think it strange that an undine would question you, given how unusual it is for an elemental to be sitting at your kitchen table."

"The thought had crossed my mind, but then I remembered that things are only strange to you if they are outside your normal experience. Being an undine is perfectly normal to you. A talking cat is not."

"I am far more than just a 'talking cat', if you don't mind." Zelda's comment caused both Hedy and Anahita to laugh, rather a bit too heartily for Zelda's taste.

"Of course, darling Zelda. You are far more than just a parlor trick. You are the Queen of our house." Hedy said quickly. Maurice gave a snicker but said nothing.

"I suppose you've forgotten about me, then." The clear, sharp voice of Alice, the magpie, could be heard from her perch near the back door.

"My apologies, Miss Alice. How could we ever forget such a lovely creature as yourself." Hedy said.

"Oh, I was only teasing. It's easy to overlook a magpie, I'm sure. I take no offense." Alice's voice was a trill of apology.

"Now, my darlings, it is time we opened the shop. I have to earn some money if we are to keep this house afloat in all the salmon, and puff pastry, and whiskey, and who knows what else, that you all require. The story of how the menagerie came to live here will have to wait."

* * *

A few hours later and Hedy was not surprised to see Mel again in the doorway, book bag slung over her shoulder. Anahita was sipping coffee at the table where Mel normally sat, so she placed her bag a few tables away.

"It's lovely to see you, Mel. Glad to have you join us again. I would like you to meet Anahita. She is a guest who will be staying with me for a bit." Mel gave Anahita a shy smile and slid into her seat, nervously pulling books out of her bag. Hedy could easily see her discomfort.

"Mel is our resident genius." Hedy said, trying to break the ice for the two strangers.

"It's nice to meet you, Mel. If someone as cosmopolitan as Hedy recommends you, that is a high compliment." Anahita flashed a smile as she spoke and Mel's face wavered between blushing and skepticism before returning the smile awkwardly.

She said very softly, "Nice to meet you also," pulling out the calculus book and furiously turning pages. Hedy brought over a Danish and a coffee, gently taking the book from Mel's hand as she did so.

"There is time enough for math, certainly. But coffee this good deserves conversation. Anahita is from Iran. She has never been to the northwest before. You two should get acquainted. Mel, why don't you sit over there. Oh, Anahita, Mel hasn't seen the staff yet." Mel looked puzzled as a knowing look passed between Hedy and the new visitor. Mel picked up her things and brought them to the other table and Hedy hoped the awkward silence would turn into conversation. Both Anahita and Mel looked like they could use a friend.

The bell tinkled and Mrs. Wilson came in, ready no doubt for more sweets for her grandchildren. She had her umbrella again, hanging carefully from her arm. Instead of her usual smile, she looked rushed and upset.

"Good morning, Mrs. Wilson. Is there something I can help you with today?" Hedy looked concerned as she wiped her hands on her polka-dot apron.

"I am babysitting my grandkids again today, Hedy. Their babysitter has gone missing and everyone is in a panic."

"Gone missing? What do you mean?" Hedy watched the woman take a breath to gather her words.

"Well, my son and his wife have a babysitter that watches the kids four days a week. She is a sweet girl, only twenty years old, and to make ends meet, she works at that coffee stand off the Auburn-Enumclaw highway, you know the one - with the bikinis." She said the word "bikinis" like it was something dirty and not spoken of in polite society.

Hedy shook her head; she had never seen a coffee stand with women in bikinis before, though she had to admit she never went to coffee stands when she could make it at home.

"It's the kind of coffee stand that young men often go to, where the girls are wearing scanty bikinis, and the coffee is very expensive. I think it is called 'Sandy Bottoms' or something like that. Or at least, it was called that. It burned to the ground late last night and Gretchen, the babysitter, was working there right before the fire. No one has seen her since." Mrs. Wilson started to cry, dabbing at the corners of her eyes with a small hanky.

"That's just terrible, Mrs. Wilson." Hedy was at a loss for what to say to comfort the woman.

"When Gretchen didn't arrive to watch the kids, they called her home and found out from her mother that she was missing. It's just awful. First, the fire at the yoga studio and now this. What in the world is happening around here? Anyway, I have to hurry over to watch the kids so their parents can get to work. Can you just pick out an assortment from the case for me? I'm at my wits' end."

Hedy picked out a mix of favorites for the children, waiving off Mrs. Wilson as she tried to pay. Mrs. Wilson nodded her thanks and picked up the box, leaving without another word; she was clearly upset with the state of the world she found herself in.

"Another fire, wow that is scary. I wonder if

there is a serial arsonist in town?" Mel said as she took out her phone to look up details on the fire. Her older sister had gone to school with Gretchen but she didn't know her herself.

Hedy shook her head, "I don't know what to think. Two late night fires in as many days. It just seems so crazy." Anahita said nothing but she instinctively grabbed the small vial at her neck again.

"Maybe this isn't a place where I should stay after all. I wouldn't have expected such dangers in a small town like this." Anahita's voice had an edge to it that sounded new to Hedy.

Before the last few days, she would have told the girl that she was silly to worry, but now, Hedy wasn't so sure.

CHAPTER SIX

"Perhaps a change of scenery would be of interest to you two. On the second floor, we have a library. I know Mel loves books and I have quite a collection of rare volumes up there. If you'd like to look around, please be my guest. It's the room at the end of the hall. Anahita can show you." Hedy wanted to take their minds off the bad news from Mrs. Wilson and for a bookworm like Mel, she expected it would be a welcome idea. She didn't know Anahita well enough to say whether it would interest her, but it had to be more interesting than sitting in the bakery, watching Hedy roll out dinner rolls, even if they were crescent shaped dragons.

"I'd love to see it. Anahita, what about you?" Mel said and Anahita nodded.

"Oh, I should mention that there is a resident spirit who likes to spend her time in that room. Her name is Adelaide. If you see the curtains rustling or feel a change in temperature, it is likely her. Don't be alarmed. She is a friendly spirit. You have to expect such things in a house this old." Hedy watched the smiles leech from their faces.

Really, why would such a thing distress anyone, Hedy thought.

"You mean a ghost? As in a haunted house kind of ghost?" Mel's voice sounded tight to Hedy, like a rubber band about to snap.

"She's a spirit, so yes, a ghost, but not in a spooky, horror movie kind of way. I wouldn't send you up there if there was any danger. I mean, come on girls, surely you aren't afraid of someone who has been dead for almost a hundred years." Hedy laughed but she was the only one.

"Uh, OK. I guess we can check it out." Mel spoke flatly and she slung her book bag over her shoulder. Anahita said nothing but led her toward the hall.

"Have fun." Hedy called out merrily to them both.

"This house, pretty weird huh?" Mel followed Anahita up the stairs, now on the other side of that strange bramble gate. She noticed a peculiar oil painting of a woman whose eyes seemed to be following her. She looked a little like Hedy, but without the white hair.

"Yes, this is a strange place, certainly. I'm not altogether sure if I am going to stay on or not. With everything I have learned today, I am re-considering my options." Anahita's hair was swaying as she walked the stairs and it caught Mel's attention; it was almost hypnotic.

"I suppose that Hedy is a bit...uh...eccentric, what with that hairdo and the retro clothes. But she seems nice and other than the fires, this town is about as sleepy as you can get. I wouldn't worry about staying here. Although this ghost, that may be another thing." Mel waited for Anahita to respond but she said nothing, instead leading her down the hallway to the library.

The door was unlocked and the smell of lavender and candlewax surrounded them. It was a small room, with just one window, but it had wall to wall bookshelves, all filled with books with cloth or leather spines. There was a small table and two wooden chairs with thick velvet cushions pushed against one wall. Mel noticed several candlesticks scattered throughout the room.

"What's with all the candles, I wonder. Seems like a weird idea with all the paper in here." Mel picked one up and gave it a sniff. It was unscented. *Wonder where the lavender scent is coming from*, she thought.

"Maybe the ghost doesn't like electricity." Anahita walked toward the table and began leafing through a book of nineteenth century recipes that Hedy must have left there. She shuddered at the description of potted meat.

Mel shrugged, though Anahita wasn't looking at her. She turned her attention to the shelves and tried to get a fix on whether things were in any particular order. It seemed like Hedy had things grouped in a general fashion, with cookbooks occupying one area, travel guides in another, history books loosely grouped by geography, and novels shelved according to height, not title or author. Squatting down, she found what looked like a scrapbook that was too tall to be placed on its edge.

She picked it up and brought it over to the table where Anahita was still wincing at the recipes, clucking in disgust at the various concoctions for gizzards and head cheese. Mel placed the book on the table, wiping away the dust from the cover as she did so. Apparently, the scrapbook wasn't something getting much use.

She opened the brown leather cover and found an old photo of a girl. Mel would have guessed she was about her own age, maybe a bit older, though it was hard to tell. The girl had pincurls around her face and she was wearing one of those hats that flappers always wore in the movies. It would be hard to know for sure, but Mel guessed that her hair was blonde. There was no way to tell the color of her wide eyes but she had a large bouquet of carnations and small white roses pressed to her chest, with the petals hitting just under her chin. She had a soft smile but there was something mischievous in her expression. The photo was held to the page with one piece of yellowing tape, clearly added later. Mel was able to lift up the bottom and read the spidery script on the back. Adelaide, aged 19.

"Check this out. I think I found the ghost. Or the girl who became a ghost." Mel held up the book slightly for Anahita to see.

"She was pretty." Anahita turned her attention to the small clipping from a newspaper that was glued to the same page, yellowed and a bit smeared. "Cherry Blossom Dance Troupe performed at the Women's Club benefit last Friday, performing an elaborate programme with costumes created and piano music played by Mrs. Olson." She squinted slightly as she read, trying to make out the aging type.

"Adelaide must have performed there. I wonder if her mother made this scrapbook for her or if she made it herself?" Mel leaned in to try to read the clipping and her arm brushed lightly against Anahita.

"What else do you see in there?" Anahita reached out with her slim brown fingers and lightly turned the page. There was a program from somewhere called The Cornish School in Seattle, which looked to be an old arts college. Next to that were more black and white photos of people in starched collars and stiff faces, none of which contained Adelaide's free-spirited face.

"This makes me too sad to look at." Mel let go of the edge of the book and turned away from the table slightly. "It feels creepy to be looking through a dead girl's memory book."

"I understand. We don't have to look at it. We don't have to stay up here either, if you don't want to. I think Hedy was just trying to give us a distraction. Have you met the other person staying here?" Mel turned back around to face Anahita and answer her question.

"Yes, I saw him yesterday. His name is Bren, I think. He looks a little like an actor or somebody famous. He's kind of handsome. Seemed OK to me. What about you? What did you think of him?"

"I met him as well. He's definitely different from anyone else I have ever met. There is something about him that seems...off. I can't explain it really, but have you ever met someone and just had a strong feeling about them from the start? He seems like he is hiding something. I suppose I shouldn't say that. I have no reason to suspect him of anything." Anahita looked at Mel for any sign of agreement on her face but there was none.

"I don't know him well enough or for long enough to have an opinion, I guess. I know what you mean about a gut feeling though, a 'spidey sense' about people my brother would call it. I usually trust my gut on that kind of thing. If I notice anything, I'll let you know." Mel was trying to be helpful and Anahita gave her a slight nod of thanks.

"Come on, we can go back downstairs. I'm not really in the mood for reading and if there is a ghost in here, she might not appreciate the company." The girls left the room, closing the door on the scents and leaving the scrapbook on the table. Neither of them noticed the curtain by the window fluttering slightly.

CHAPTER SEVEN

It was late afternoon before Hedy saw Bren, though she was busy enough with customers all day that perhaps he had been down earlier in the kitchen and she just didn't notice him. Much to Hedy's delight, Anahita and Mel had decided to go for a walk around town and they weren't back yet. To Hedy's mind, Mel seemed like a girl who could use more friends outside of a book and she hoped they were hitting it off. When Hedy finally saw Bren, he looked tired to her, and she suspected his late night activity was to blame. She felt that wiggle of doubt in the back of her brain creep out.

"I heard you were out and about last night. Anything interesting going on?" Hedy inquired as Bren sipped his coffee as he leaned against the counter.

"I've always been a night person but last night I was out because there is something going on in this town. Something bad."

"Are you talking about the fires?" Hedy asked. Bren nodded his head; clearly, he knew there had been a second one.

"Yes, it's that but there is more to it than that. Something just feels wrong. I'm not a psychic but

I have been feeling a presence ever since I came to town. Last night, I went looking." He took another sip of coffee.

"What did you find?" Hedy studied his face as he spoke and she could see him searching for the words.

"I walked to the scene of the first fire, it wasn't hard to find. I tried to find anything that would give me some hints as to the source. Fire smells different to a salamander - we can tell what causes it, if it is natural or man-made, things that are hard to put into words. The fire at the studio was definitely arson but the rapture of arson was missing, if that makes sense." He saw Hedy's confusion on her face.

"The rapture of arson? What does that mean?" Hedy had never heard such an expression.

"It's hard to explain. Arson, as awful as it is, brings a perverse joy to the arsonist and I can smell that joy, that rapture, the *verzückung* in the fire. This fire had none of that - it was set on purpose but it wasn't for the joy of the arsonist, it was for another reason. As I said, it is hard to explain."

"Well, that makes sense I guess, as the owner is missing, so perhaps the fire was set to hide her disappearance, not for the sake of the fire itself." Hedy had never considered that arson could be a form of joy and the thought made her shiver.

"That may be true but I think there is more to it than that. I think the fire was also meant to cleanse, like some kind of purging."

"Did you see the second fire? I heard it was at a coffee stand just outside of town." Hedy watched him take another sip before he answered, his eyes lingering on the lip of the cup, avoiding her gaze.

"I saw the fire and smoke, I even smelled the spark as it was lit, but on foot I was too far away to make it there before it was all over. Again, the fire smelled of hate and purging, no arsonist's joy."

"Well, I must say you look exhausted. I expect you would be with running all over town on foot in the dead of night. You could have borrowed my car, you know. Rest up - your visit with us is supposed to be restorative for your journey and you look like ten miles of bumpy road right now." Bren laughed and nodded his head.

"Yes, no doubt I've looked better. I thought I would get a book from the library, if Adelaide wouldn't mind, and just relax in my room for a bit. I know I haven't been the ideal guest..."

"Nonsense, your time is your own. Feel free to do just as you planned." The front door bell tinkled again. "As you can see, today is quite busy with customers so I will stay busy." Bren nodded and retreated back toward the kitchen and the back stairway.

"Isn't it perfect? It's exactly what we were looking for." The woman was gesturing broadly to the two other women who were with her. All three were dressed in various black layers and silver jewelry pieces.

"Good afternoon, ladies. How can I help you?"

The woman who had spoken seemed to be in charge of the group and she stepped up toward the counter.

"We were wondering if you ever rent out your shop for small groups?" The woman had an intensity about her that Hedy found intriguing. *She must be the leader*, Hedy thought.

"Well, yes, I informally let groups such as a local knitting club or garden group hold monthly meetings, but the shop stays open during their visits. Are you talking about closing things up for a private meeting?" The three women nodded in unison. "Well, I haven't done that before but I suppose if the time were right, I would be willing. What were you thinking?"

The intense woman looked rapturous as she spoke. "The new moon is tonight and it would be the perfect night for our group to practice our connection to the spirit world. Your house has a reputation for being haunted, did you know that?"

Hedy smiled broadly and nodded. "Yes, I've heard that."

"I know it is short notice, but we were hoping you wouldn't mind closing shop early tonight and allowing us to rent out your space for a bit. It would mean a great deal to our group if you would." The woman looked at Hedy as if her life depended on the answer.

"Well, I suppose that would be alright. Normally, I close up later in the evening, depending on whether there are customers coming by, but I could close up by eight o'clock, would that work for you?"

"Oh yes, that would be perfect. There will be six of us and we would pay you for your time. We won't be any trouble, I assure you. We are hardly a rowdy bunch." The other two women chuckled lightly at the suggestion.

"It sounds like a plan then. I'll see you back here around eight." The women were visibly pleased and they swept out the door in a flurry of black. They were hardly through the doorway when Anahita and Mel came back in, their faces flushed.

"Well, looks like you two had a brisk walk, your faces are ruddy." Hedy filled two glasses with ice water from the carafe and placed them on the counter.

"Yes, we practically ran back. We have some news." Mel paused for a moment to take a sip of water before continuing. "We walked over to where the coffee stand used to be, to see what was happening there. We met up with one of the girls who used to work there, the one that worked last night just as Gretchen was coming on shift. Jenny is her name." Mel paused again and took another sip. It had been a while since she had trained in track and her cardio had suffered for it.

"Jenny remembers a man who bought a coffee right as Gretchen started working. She remembered him because he had a German accent and reddish brown hair. Who does that sound like?"

Anahita said, giving Hedy a look.

"The man was asking questions, wanting to know how late the stand was open, did the girls work alone there, were there any surveillance cameras, things like that. Jenny also noticed he was on foot, which is odd for the coffee stand, since it is on the outskirts of town and all the customers normally drive up." Anahita reported.

"Jenny said she told all this to the police earlier." Mel chimed back in now that she had her breath back.

"And you both think that this man was Bren?" Hedy looked at the girls and Anahita gave a small nod for both of them.

"I will talk to him about this, although I can tell you that earlier he said the reason he was out so late was he was trying to learn more about the fire at the yoga studio. Mel, I should explain that Bren has a way about him when it comes to fire, he has special knowledge, like an investigator you might say, so he says he thought he could be of some help." Hedy thought they both looked skeptical, especially Anahita.

"Well, that all may be true but it certainly seems strange that he happened to be at the coffee stand just a short while before the second fire started, I mean what are the odds of that?" Mel speculated over the staggeringly small odds.

"As I said, I will speak with him, but for now, perhaps you two might be willing to help me out in the kitchen. We're having pasta in a pumpkin béchamel sauce for dinner and the roasted pumpkin is ready to be peeled and mashed. Mel, you are welcome to stay for dinner if you like." Hedy thought her voice sounded a bit sharp and she realized she was irritated. She had a nagging feeling that Bren had lied to her and the one thing she hated the most was a liar.

"Oh, that is very nice, Hedy, but I need to get home and check in with my mom. I'll give Anahita a hand in the kitchen though before I go." Mel smiled at Anahita, who looked disappointed that Mel wouldn't be staying.

"Not to worry, Anahita - I have a feeling we will be seeing Mel again tomorrow morning. You two can continue your amateur sleuthing then." The girls headed back to the kitchen, leaving Hedy alone with her thoughts.

It seemed significant that Bren hadn't mentioned his visit to the coffee stand; he clearly had the opportunity to tell her and he didn't. The yoga studio and the coffee stand were quite a distance apart, not easy on foot. *What would have drawn him that far out of town before the fire started?* Hedy had more questions than answers, and she wasn't quite sure how to ask her guest without accusing him of something awful. The unease in her gut sat there heavy.

The girls were out of earshot and there were no customers around. Hedy did something she had never tried before. She called out to Adelaide to ask for help.

"Adelaide. I'd like to speak with you. About your warnings. About Bren." Hedy felt foolish speaking this loudly, as if the ghost couldn't hear her unless she shouted toward the library. She didn't know for sure but she guessed that Adelaide could hear her from where ever she was in the house.

"Adelaide. I know you tried to warn me and I know I brushed you off. But please, if you know something, can you tell me? I'm sorry that I scolded you earlier." She didn't know if the ghost would hold a grudge or not, but she hoped spirits would be above such petty human behavior.

"Adelaide? Can you hear me?" Hedy stopped. If Adelaide wanted to appear, she would have. Maybe she was punishing Hedy for taking her to task earlier.

"Of all the ghosts in the world, I have to share the house with one who pouts." Hedy whispered under her breath. Across the room, a small crystal salt dish tumbled and broke against the hardwood floor.

"Adelaide? Was that you? If it was, I'm sorry I said that you pout. I'm just having a hard time right now and could use your help." Hedy spoke again into the emptiness of the shop but there was nothing speaking back. *Now, in addition to my worries, I have a mess to clean up,* she thought as she picked up a small whisk and dustpan. *Petulant ghost,* she thought, without daring again to say the words out loud.

CHAPTER EIGHT

Dinner was a quiet affair. Bren was still upstairs and Mel had left to go home, leaving Anahita and Hedy alone with the menagerie. Hedy tried her best to make small talk with the girl, asking her about her home in Iran and general questions to see if she would share the purpose of her travels, but Anahita wasn't saying much. She seemed preoccupied and lost in her own thoughts. After helping with the dishes, she asked Hedy if she could be excused to her room.

"I'm eager for a soak in the tub. I need to replenish myself." Hedy had noticed that the girl looked a bit more pallid than she had earlier in the day, but Hedy had chalked that up to a day of walking around town and looking for clues. Perhaps it was something more.

"By all means, my dear. The tub is yours. You'll find towels on the étagère in the corner, along with any bath salts you might need."

"No salts required for me. Just a drop of the waters from my home, from Ovan Lake, is all I need." She held the filigree bottle at her neck and gave Hedy a smile. "I'll be up bright and early to help you in the shop, if that is alright."

"It certainly is. Thank you, Anahita. Good night. I'm glad you and Mel hit it off." The girl smiled and said good night as she passed through the kitchen on her way upstairs.

* * *

Hedy had almost forgotten the arrangement to close early when she heard the bell tinkle just before eight o'clock. She walked out from the kitchen and found six women, ranging from late twenties to early sixties, by Hedy's guess, arranged in a half moon shape in front of the counter.

"Good evening. We're here." The leader of the group smiled and passed several twenty-dollar bills across the counter. "We never discussed price, I hope this is sufficient."

Hedy accepted the money and placed it in her apron pocket. "Oh, that is fine, thank you. Feel free to use any table you wish, I will close the front door for any further customers."

The women took the one circular table that Hedy had in the shop and began setting up their supplies. A tablecloth, speckled in silver moons and stars came out of a bag on which was printed 'My other car is a broom'. Larger pillar candles were placed just off center, next to a small crystal bowl containing some kind of powdered herb or incense.

"Is there a way to dim the lights in here? I supposed I should have asked that before. Bright artificial light isn't conducive. You might not know this, but spirits do not like electricity." The leader said as Hedy went to the small panel of push button switches on the wall, smiling as she did so. She was familiar with that bit of ghost trivia. Hedy pressed two of the buttons and the lights were dimmed, leaving the room mostly in shadow.

"Perfect, thank you."

Hedy had no particular opinion about those who wanted to make contact with the spirits; after all, she herself now lived with a ghost, so it seemed like a reasonable activity for those so inclined. She did find the pomp and circumstance of this group of women to be a bit theatrical. All the black trappings and moon imagery seemed a bit like a stereotype out of a movie. The witches she had known were usually solitary types, more kitchen witches or herbalists than those embracing the black pointed hat. Most of the witches she had met had been in New Orleans, so there had been a few who embraced the spectacle. *Like Anita,* Hedy thought, with a wince. She exited the shop and found a quiet corner in the entry to review some old recipes she had found in an antique shop. She did not want to take that trip down memory lane at the moment; too many painful memories.

The women had apparently lit their candles because Hedy could see the soft glow of candlelight coming through the archway from the shop. She heard faint murmuring as they began to chant, though the words weren't really audible. The chanting continued, rising in pitch and volume, and she saw the candlelight flickering as if being fluttered by a breeze. Adelaide was likely nearby. *Could the women sense it,* she wondered.

Hedy considered whether she should have mentioned Adelaide to the women. They had suggested the house was haunted but she hadn't confirmed that Adelaide was a full presence that made herself known. Partly she hadn't said anything because Adelaide, even in spirit form, had the freedom to appear or not, and certainly not on Hedy's command, if today was any indication. If she had mentioned Adelaide to the group, they would have expected to meet her and might have been disappointed by the outcome. But there was more to it than that. Hedy had to admit that she wasn't taking the women and their efforts that seriously, and it surprised her that she was judging their worth by their appearance. She honestly hadn't expected them to make contact with any spirit, even Adelaide.

"Well, that's rather a rotten attitude, old girl. I would have expected better from someone of your maturity and experience." Hedy murmured to herself and made a note to do better in the future. It was then that she heard the scream.

She hurried into the shop and saw the women gathered around the table, their hands joined together in a ring. Near the edge of the table was

Adelaide, fully visible in the flickering candlelight. One of the women had given the scream but they were all silent now, looking at each other in helpless wonder.

"This is Adelaide. She lives in the house." Hedy said calmly, thinking perhaps a proper introduction might help the women feel more at ease with the spirit hovering above the table. Adelaide gazed around the circle before looking directly at the leader of the group.

"She wants you to speak, Helen." The woman nearest to the leader stage whispered and gave a soft tap with her elbow into Helen's side.

"Yes, alright. I will." Helen muttered reluctantly before she spoke in her full voice. "Adelaide, thank you for joining our circle. We wish to learn more about you and what it is like on the other side. Tell us your story, dear spirit." Even afraid, Helen seemed to have a flair for the dramatic and her former intensity was coming back.

Hedy watched as Adelaide shimmered in and out of focus, as if she were deciding whether to stay or to leave. Hedy herself only knew bits and pieces of Adelaide's story; the ghost had not spoken about her past and when she did speak, it was usually only in riddles. Hedy had found an old scrapbook in the library but there wasn't much in there to go one.

"Within these walls I was born. Within these walls I died. Within these walls I must remain." Adelaide's voice was raspy, like dried husks scraping out the sound, but not unpleasant to hear. She spoke more like shuffled paper or hissing tea kettles. The candles continued to flicker though there was no wind in the room. Her form had a faint bluish tinge.

"How did you die, Adelaide. Please tell us." Helen spoke again, her hands were gripping the hands of the women on either side of her. Hedy could see their white knuckles.

Again, Adelaide paused for a bit, shimmering in and out of focus. Her voice finally broke the stillness. "A flower in bloom, too bold and sweetly scented, plucked by the one who keeps a stern garden, a stem crushed." Hedy tried to make sense of the riddle. *If Adelaide was the bloom that was plucked, who was the stern garden keeper? A stem crushed?*

"Can you tell us who did this to you?" Another woman spoke up and Helen gave her a sharp look. Clearly, Helen was the speaker for the circle.

"No friend to me, no friend to Eve, no friend indeed. Dark hearted and seeker of sin, preacher of chastity." Adelaide began to fade, her voice trailed behind her as she spoke. "Sins of the father, curse of the son, woe for the mothers and daughters now gone."

The circle waited a few moments before releasing their hands and their breath. Adelaide was gone.

"That was incredible. Wasn't that incredible, Helen?" Several women were murmuring their disbelief.

"It was more than we could have hoped for. To see her appear and hear her voice from the beyond. Amazing. Beyond words. A full apparition." Helen rose from her chair and looked around the circle. "We have experienced something amazing tonight, sisters. We must close the circle and bless the four corners for what we have learned."

Hedy started to leave the entryway, wanting to give them their privacy to conclude their ceremony when the youngest of the group spoke up.

"Did you know she was strangled, Adelaide, I mean? I read about it online, on a local haunted history page." The others in the circle looked at the young woman, waiting for more. "She was strangled here in her own home, back in the early 1920s, with a long gold necklace that was wrapped around her throat. They never found the killer."

Hedy felt a weight on her shoulders, to think of a young Adelaide murdered in her own home. It must have been terrifying for her. She went back to the entry teary-eyed while the circle chanted softly behind her. A murderer had left behind Adelaide's spirit, trapped in the house.

CHAPTER NINE

"Thank you again for letting us use your shop for our gathering. Meeting Adelaide was a rare treat and we certainly look forward to coming back again soon." Helen shook hands with Hedy as the women filed out of shop. "I suspect you knew we would meet her tonight, didn't you?"

"Honestly, I did not know if she would appear or not. She has her own will and does as she pleases, like any teenager then or now. I will say that she has never said that much to me about what happened to her, so I thank you for what I learned tonight. It has given me much to think about." The ladies shuffled out and Hedy closed the door behind them, latching the bolt. It was going on ten o'clock and Hedy was bone weary.

"Well, that was quite the soirée, was it not?" Maurice had been observing everything from a dark corner in the entry, perched comfortably on a velvet pillow.

"Indeed. Now we know a bit more about Adelaide than we did before, which I suppose is a good thing. I hate to think of her dying in this house though. I suppose I could have just assumed that since she haunts this place, but you know me, I don't like to dwell on the negative. I guess I assumed it was natural causes, not murder." Hedy began turning off the lights and drawing the curtains.

"If Adelaide hadn't wished to speak, those women wouldn't have raised so much as a whisper from any ghost. You know I am the last to judge, but honestly, they wouldn't have made contact with anyone with a room full of Ouija boards. Adelaide wanted to speak."

"Maurice, I caught myself thinking the same thing about the women and it isn't our place to judge, but you may be right about Adelaide wishing to be heard. I tried talking to her earlier but she must still be angry with me. She has been disturbed since Bren's arrival and now tonight, she is speaking in riddles about her passing. She definitely has something on her mind." Maurice followed Hedy as she made her way to the stairs; she offered a hand to him and he climbed up, grateful for a ride up the many stairs to the third floor. Maurice was not a young chinchilla, though he would never admit that.

"Perhaps she will tell you more of the story tomorrow. In any event, what are you going to do about the salamander? Do we need to worry? Two fires as soon as he comes to town seems a bit too coincidental." Hedy was quiet for a few steps before answering the chinchilla.

"I honestly don't know, Maurice." They made

the rest of the climb to the third floor in silence. Maurice hopped down at the top of the stairs and made his way into the cozy burrow he had created in the corner behind a wing back chair. Hedy bid him good night and headed into her own room.

Hedy had claimed the full attic as her bedroom as soon as moving into the house, although it had required the addition of a bathroom. She loved the angled ceilings and dormer windows, the small rise of steps that led to a large open space. The space suited her well, with her bed juxtaposed against one of the angled walls, an expansive wardrobe instead of a standard closet, and a cozy loveseat with a stack of books begging to be read. It was her favorite room in the house, even more than the kitchen, and that was saying something. Normally, it was a refuge from anything and everything; the menagerie was under strict instruction to stay out of the room. This was Hedy's oasis.

But tonight, her room gave her no rest. She sat on the edge of her bed and chewed thoughtfully on her thumbnail. She liked a house in order - unusual, strange, even peculiar was fine, but ultimately there was order. Right now, her house was definitely not in order.

"This is ridiculous. I am just going to talk with him and get to the bottom of this tonight." Hedy slipped on her dressing gown and headed back down to the second floor. Zelda was sleeping, or doing a good impression of sleep, in a chair placed between Bren's room and Anahita's. Hedy gave a soft rap on the door with her knuckles and waited to hear movement. She knocked again and still she heard nothing.

"He's not in there." Zelda murmured quietly before curling back up.

Hedy tried the knob and it twisted easily. She entered the room and immediately was struck by the strong smell of smoke and ash. The clothes resting on a small footstool near the door were the source of the smell. No doubt these were what Bren had worn when he was exploring the site of the first fire. *She would offer to wash them tomorrow*, she thought.

Otherwise, the room look mostly undisturbed. The bed had not been slept in, which didn't surprise her. The whole purpose of the stone chaise lounge was to give him a place to rest that was not combustible. She felt the stone and it was warm to the touch. Turning to exit the room, she noticed a bright pink disposable coffee cup in the trash by the bathroom. Picking it up, she could easily read *Sandy Bottoms* with a lipstick kiss print, stamped on the side.

"It was terrible coffee and they charged six dollars for it." Bren was standing in the doorway, holding a plate of leftover pasta.

"Oh, yes, sorry. I'm not spying in your room, really. Well, I am, but unintentionally, I promise. I came down to speak with you and you weren't here." She placed the cup back into the garbage can.

"I have no secrets. Well, at least none that would be found out in a small wastebasket. I missed dinner so I thought I would fix myself a plate." He came into the room and set the plate on the edge of the dresser.

"No, that's fine. Really. Again, I'm sorry to be in here without you. I just had something on my mind and I guess that made me lose my better judgment. I'll leave you to your dinner." She headed toward the door but he was blocking the entrance.

"No, please don't go. You have questions, please let me answer them. I prefer no secrets or doubts between us. You want to know why I have the coffee cup from the stand in my garbage." Hedy felt so awkward but she needed to ask him what she came for.

"Well, yes, although I didn't know about the cup when I came down here. I heard that someone who fit your description was seen at the coffee stand before it burned down and they were asking questions, questions that sounded strange in light of the fire. I wanted to know if it was you."

"Hedy, everything I told you before was true. What I didn't tell you was I actually went to the coffee stand before I went to the site of the first fire. I went there not because I wanted to set it on fire, but because I could smell the danger around the place. It sounds crazy, well crazier than anything else I have told you, but I didn't want you to think I was some kind of... crackpot, yes that's the word."

Hedy looked at him and wanted to believe him but she couldn't quite manage to keep the skepticism off her face.

"I know, it does sound crazy. That's why I didn't tell you. Let me try to explain." He gestured for her to sit down and she perched on the edge of the bed. He was still between her and the doorway.

"Salamanders can smell fire, as I've told you. Elementals in general have a deep connection to their element and they can see and smell and even taste things that relate to it. All that is true. But for me, I seem to have a sixth sense that is even rare among salamanders. I can smell fire before it even starts, before match strikes tinder, before the first flickers begin. If a place is soon to be consumed by fire, I can smell it. I say smell but it really isn't that - you can't really smell something that hasn't happened yet. But that is the closest I can call it and have it make sense for you. I breathe in the danger and I just know that it is coming."

"And that is what happened last night? You could smell that the coffee stand was in danger? If that is true, why didn't you warn the girls working there?" She was starting to get angry to think that Bren could have prevented the tragedy and did nothing.

"You know what I am and you don't believe me, do you think those girls would believe me? Also, I can't pinpoint exactly when something is going to happen, only that danger is there. That is why I went and asked about security or people lurking around. I even stayed nearby, watching to see if anything looked amiss but there was nothing. I decided to use the time to check out the first fire and hope that maybe it would give me a clue that I could use to prevent whatever was coming, whenever that was. I was wrong, clearly." Bren came over to the bed and sat next to Hedy.

"I feel terrible, Hedy. Truly. Now you know why I want to end this curse that hangs over me and my life. Everywhere I go, I find danger of fire in the wind and it haunts me. If I could have saved the girl or stopped the fire, don't you think I would have done it?" His voice sounded strained, almost pleading.

Hedy looked at Bren, scanning his brown eyes to see if she could see the truth in them. Adelaide was right, there was smoke around him. She couldn't tell if what he said was true or not. Her gut instinct, usually spot on about people, was silent.

"Bren, if what you say is true, you bear a terrible burden and I can understand why you wish to be free of it. You have to understand though that the girl you met, the girl who made you that terrible coffee, is gone. There is no sign of her and likely something awful has happened to her. If there is any way you can help, I think you should. Part of your curse is that it brings responsibility."

Hedy stood up and left him alone in the room; he didn't try to stop her. It wasn't her place to lecture him but his decision to leave the coffee stand unguarded likely left the girl to the very danger he knew was lurking. Bren wasn't to blame for the fire or the disappearance of the girl, at least as far as Hedy knew, but in Hedy's eyes, he hadn't done all he could have to prevent it and she didn't know how to reconcile that. She climbed the stairs to the attic not feeling any better than when she came down them. It would be a long night for both of them.

CHAPTER TEN

The first hints of clouds were waiting for Hedy as she faced the morning. They may not have held rain but they were a sign that the sunny October days would be drawing to a close. Maybe they were a sign of other things too, since Hedy's mind was clouded from a night of little sleep. To top it off, Mr. Jeffries was also waiting for her on the front porch when she opened the shop.

"Good morning, Mr. Jeffries. What brings you..."

"I thought we had an understanding about the yard. Weren't you going to be bringing in a gardener? The leaves are back and the gardens that face my house are a disaster. I shouldn't have to look at that rubbish."

Hedy was in no mood for humoring his rudeness. "Sir, I will tend to my garden as I see fit. As I told you, I will be contacting a gardener, and I will. It will be on my timeline, not yours. Unless you have anything else to discuss, I need to open my shop."

"Hedy, is everything alright?" Anahita had come up behind her and was standing near her elbow by the door. Jeffries gave the girl a withering look.

"What are you running, a hotel? The city has ordinances against hotels in residential areas, you know." Jeffries' blotchy face was turning a lovely shade of purple.

"Not at all, Mr. Jeffries. Just houseguests for no compensation, nothing remotely illegal about that. But feel free to try again, what else do you have this morning?" Hedy knew she shouldn't be goading the man but she had had her fill of his nosy neighbor routine.

"If people like you would have some decency and behave like you ought to, this world would be a better place. We don't need your kind of sloppy and freewheeling living."

"That's enough, sir. This conversation is over." Hedy firmly shut the door in his face, leaving him sputtering and apoplectic on the front porch.

"So much for 'love your neighbor', huh? I should have taken the high road but honestly, it is much too early for that much stupidity and rancor. Lack of sleep has not helped my disposition." Hedy sighed dramatically. Anahita chuckled, which caused Hedy to laugh as well. "And to show that I am more than just an indecent, sloppy, freewheeling garden destroying 'kind', I'll even call the gardener today." They both headed into the kitchen to get coffee and put Mr. Jeffries and his demands out of their minds.

"Good morning, ladies. There is a delivery on the back porch, Hedy." Alice trilled her words rather fetchingly, clearly feeling chipper on a cloudy morning and excited to have some news to share. Hedy knew that the bird always wanted to be helpful.

"Thank you, Alice. It must be the bushel of apples I ordered from the farmstand last week. The Honeycrisps must be ready." Hedy popped open the back door and sure enough, a large box of apples was there. "That certainly puts a better spin on the day. I think some poison apple pie might be just the thing - do you think Mr. Jeffries would like a slice?" Hedy grabbed the handle and dragged the box into the kitchen. She gave the door a kick with her foot but it didn't quite latch shut.

"Real poison or just one of your peculiarities?" Anahita said as she came over and helped Hedy lift the large box onto the kitchen table. Hedy thought the girl was joking but there looked like a tiny bit of doubt on her face. That amused her.

"I suppose not real poison, though it would be a little tempting." The front door bell tinkled; Hedy had forgotten to lock it. "That will be Mel, I think." Anahita gave Hedy a smile and headed into the shop.

"I think those two like each other, wouldn't you say? I'm not the brightest bird, I know, but even I can see that." Alice trilled again from her perch and Hedy nodded back. Hedy scooped up several Honeycrisp apples and placed them in the bowl with the Granny Smiths she already had.

"There is a connection there. Time will tell if it

is friendship or something more." Hedy smiled at Alice as she picked up the bowl brimming with fresh apples. There were few things in the world that Hedy loved more than in-season apples.

"Girls, would you like to make a poison apple pie?" She carried the bowl into the shop, leaving the back door ajar behind her.

Though a few early morning customers interrupted the pie crust lesson, both girls had an opportunity to learn how to properly make a lard pie crust. It was a bit finicky for first-timers, but under Hedy's watchful gaze, both mastered rolling it out with a minimal amount of handling.

"Very good, that looks perfect. Now, loosely roll it back onto your rolling pin and use it to carry it to your pie pan. Yes, like that. You both are naturals." The girls smiled and Hedy helped them flute the edges of the crust until they had two customer-worthy pie crusts, waiting for the filling.

"My mom would never believe I made a pie crust from scratch. Baking in our house might happen if we have some of those crescent rolls in a tube or prefab cookie dough. What about you, Ana?"

"Definitely no baking in my family. I'm not sure what my mother would say about this." Anahita's face was smiling but Hedy heard a slight hesitation in her voice.

"Hedy, do you know there is a fox in the kitchen?" Maurice had joined them in the shop and made his way to the top of the counter. He said the word 'fox' with a thick varnish of disdain.

"Uh, did you just hear that?" Mel's face was stricken in surprise and fear and her voice was a shriek. "Did that chinchilla just speak?"

Anahita and Hedy looked at each other with worried looks. This was Mel's first time hearing one of the members of the menagerie.

"My dear, don't worry. I can explain everything, I really can. But first, I need to see to the fox in the kitchen." Hedy gave Anahita a nod, indicating she should watch over Mel while Hedy dealt with the intruder.

Just as Maurice had said, there was a fox over by the potbelly stove. The creature didn't seem afraid when Hedy entered the room, and instead seemed to be warming himself.

"Hello there. I see I must have left the backdoor open. I hope you are a friendly fox and not going to cause any trouble." Hedy spoke out loud, mostly for herself, but just in case the fox understood her. She didn't know if the staff in the hallway would have any effect on a wild creature wandering into the house. Alice was nowhere to be seen. Hopefully he hadn't had a magpie snack.

The fox looked at her curiously, his fluffy white tipped tail coiled around his feet. With a tilt of his head, he turned and headed silently and slowly back toward the door.

"Thank you." Hedy gave a small sigh as she watched the fox cross the threshold.

The fox turned back to look at her before heading for the stairs. “My name is Ren. Never heard a human speak before, didn’t know they could. Huh, imagine that. Wait until the missus hears.” With that, he was gone.

Hedy came back into the shop to find the girls gone. She checked the entry and found them in front of the staff on the wall. Anahita was explaining the story to Mel.

“So, you're telling me that animals in this house can speak because of this stick?” Mel gestured toward the staff and Anahita nodded.

“That’s what she says. Though I haven’t ruled out that she is a witch. That makes more sense, really.”

“I’m not a witch, Anahita. At least not by training, though it might be in my blood. If you had been in the kitchen with me with the fox, you would have had another example of the staff having an effect on animals. Apparently even wild animals who wander inside can be affected.” Hedy filed that tidbit away in her mind. The dealer she had purchased the staff from way back when hadn’t mentioned any of this.

“Incredible. It is amazing. Do you know how much money you could make by showing this to the world? You are a regular Dr. Doolittle!” Mel said with amazement. Hedy looked quizzically at Mel and Anahita shrugged her shoulders; neither knew the reference.

“Look, Mel. You can’t tell anyone about the staff. It would be dangerous for the animals, and frankly dangerous for me. People fear what they don't understand and before you know it, things could get ugly. Can I count on you to keep this secret?" Hedy looked at Mel, hoping the girl understood just how dangerous such knowledge could be. She really needed to be able to trust her with this secret.

"Oh, of course, I won't say a word. I mean, who would believe me? I can't believe it and I heard it for myself. Can we go talk to him some more?" Mel sounded excited at the prospect.

"Well, you can try. You might get him into a conversation if you ask him about his book on Proust." Both girls looked shocked at Hedy's statement.

"Yes, I forgot to mention. They can read as well."

CHAPTER ELEVEN

True to her word, Hedy called the gardener she had located on the ad in the grocery store. At least, she thought she had called the gardener. The person on the other end of the phone had a thick Scottish accent and quite possibly the world's worst cell phone, combining into a difficult conversation at best. She thought they had agreed to meet at the shop and discuss the bid around noon.

The girls had tried in vain to get Maurice to be more communicative, so they were off in search of Zelda. Bren, true to form, hadn't made an appearance this morning, though given how they left things last night, she wasn't sure what would be the state of things when he did show up.

The bell signaled the door and Hedy looked up to find a woman standing in the doorway. Rather than enter the shop, she hovered in the entry, looking at the walls and artifacts with obvious fascination.

"Good morning, can I help you?" Hedy came around the counter to close the gap but the woman never turned her head to acknowledge her.

"So, this is the place." The woman spoke softly, so close to a whisper that Hedy wasn't sure she had heard the woman at all.

"Pardon me, did you say something?" Hedy came closer to her but stopped just out of arm's reach.

"Not at all what I expected, to be sure." The woman spoke again, still not looking toward Hedy, but rather stepping lightly into the entry and toward the stairway.

"The shop is back this way. Perhaps if I knew what you were looking for, I could be of some assistance." Hedy stepped into the entry and watched the woman examine the objects and paintings closely.

"Indeed, what I am looking for is always the same thing." The woman finally turned to face Hedy, "But sometimes, I happen on a very special place, such as this town." Her eyes were very dark, with hardly a rim of white around the edges. She smiled but it had no warmth at all, only menace.

"Enumclaw is a nice town, certainly." Hedy didn't know what else to say. The woman's gaze prickled the skin on Hedy's neck. Her eyes were not natural and Hedy couldn't look away.

"Special to be sure, but hardly 'nice'. No doubt you know about the fires and the women who have gone missing. Nothing very 'nice' about that, wouldn't you say?" The woman came closer to

Hedy and it was all she could do not to back away from her. Hedy's gut was telling her to get away.

"You are special too, aren't you? You and this house, and the people and things in it. All very special, very precious. I must say, it makes my days much more interesting when there are special people such as yourselves in my path." Her voice had hardly risen above a whisper.

Hedy wanted to tell the woman to leave the house but her mouth wasn't moving. The woman headed toward the door, unasked. "I will be seeing you again, I am sure, you and your lovely house, and your *special* friends. It's nice to meet you in person. You may call me Lyssa, Miss Leckermaul." The woman was gone.

Hedy was not one for taking a sip of spirits early in the day but she poured a small bit of whiskey into her coffee cup. She had no idea what had just happened.

"Hedy, are you alright?" Mel and Ana had returned from their search for Zelda and both girls looked worried. "Your face has gone white as your hair."

"I'm alright, just a very strange and unsettling visitor. And not Mr. Jeffries this time. A woman, a weird woman, with these weird eyes." The girls came up to the counter and Ana gave a sniff at the whiff of whiskey she smelled coming from the coffee cup.

"This woman came into the house, and just stayed in the entryway, looking at the walls and things. She hardly spoke above a whisper and she made strange statements about how 'special' we all were, not 'nice' but 'special' and how special Enumclaw was. She had these dark eyes, almost black, like they were all iris. I tried to tell her to leave but the words wouldn't come out." Hedy considered herself of hardy stock but she was shaken.

"I wonder what she meant by 'special'? What is so special about this town?" Anahita looked at Mel, thinking maybe she knew something that the other two did not.

"Enumclaw is just a run of the mill small town. Nothing overly special as far as I know. It's close to Mount Rainier and it has fierce windstorms some times. The whole plateau is an old lava flow from the volcano, which I guess is kinda special. But honestly, I don't know what she is talking about." Mel was searching her brain for any tidbits from her freshman Washington history class that might be useful.

"What does the name 'Enumclaw' mean? I've never heard such a name before." Anahita had found the name curious when she had first learned it was the site of a waystation on her journey.

"If I remember right, the word comes from the Salish people and it means 'place of evil spirits' or something like that. I think it has something to do with Mount Enumclaw, which is just outside of town." She'd lived in Enumclaw her whole life but she had never felt the urge to go check out the mountain. She wasn't especially outdoorsy and even if she were, there were more interesting places to check out.

"The woman, she called herself Lyssa, said it made her days more interesting when there were special people about."

"Did you say Lyssa? Her name was Lyssa? And you said she had very dark eyes?" Anahita's face visibly blanched.

"Yes, her eyes were almost black, almost to the edges. Why? Who was she?"

"I can't believe it but I think you just met the goddess of rage and madness, Hedy."

"Anahita, what are you talking about?" Hedy was in no mood for games right now.

"No, hear me out. The name of Lyssa is known throughout the Mediterranean and Middle East as the name of the ancient Greek goddess of rage and madness. Legend has it that she is the child of Nyx, goddess of the night and that is why she has eyes of darkness. She travels the world sowing seeds of frenzy and hate, leaving destruction in her wake." Anahita thought of the stories her grandmother would tell, the ancient Persian words echoing in her head.

"But why would she be here, assuming a 'goddess' could be alive and well in the 21st century." Mel had already had a day where she learned that animals in the house could talk; taking on the theory of a living, breathing goddess was a bit much.

"She said she only ever has one thing she wants,

though she didn't tell me what that was." Hedy tried to remember if there was anything else that Lyssa had told her, but that was all she could recall.

"She is endlessly traveling the world, bringing rage in her wake. Why she would come to Enumclaw, I can't say, but if she really is Lyssa, there is danger coming for sure." Ana placed her hand on Mel's and gave it a squeeze. Mel smiled and then blushed.

"Who is coming and bringing danger?" Bren had come into the shop unnoticed. His voice sounded sharp.

"Hedy had a visit this morning from a woman named Lyssa. From how she described her, she sounds like the Lyssa of legend. One who brings rage and madness." Anahita said.

"Rage and madness, and rabies in animals, I've heard the legends. But they are just that, legends. Why on earth would a goddess be roaming the farmland of Enumclaw? It sounds unlikely, wouldn't you say?" Bren sounded like he was trying to explain away Ana's theory.

"Why not here? She travels the world and looks for places to sow the seeds of discord, to bring rage and anger to her followers. What better place than America right now, with all the fear of others that seems to be growing. Small towns are just the sort of place to stir things up, in a community that is close and connected." Ana had a quiet strength about her and this was the first time Hedy had heard her really raise her voice.

"OK, fair enough, maybe it was *the* Lyssa of legend. I don't think it does much good to be borrowing trouble or making assumptions, but whether you met an old and powerful goddess or just a strange woman, the fact remains there *is* something happening in this town. Someone is setting fires and taking women." Bren said and Hedy wondered if he could see the distrust in Ana's eyes.

"You are right, Bren. Enough with speculating. Enough with guessing. There is nothing we can do about any of this right now. I am going to focus on what I can change, and that is getting a gardener, and tending the shop, and being a host for travelers. Beyond that, the world is going to have to take care of itself for right now." Hedy walked away from the counter and into the kitchen, leaving the three of them alone.

"I don't know her well but I think Hedy is scared. That didn't sound like her just then." Mel spoke up for the first time in a while.

"Sometimes it is smart to be scared. And these are scary times, especially for someone like Hedy - a person who isn't like everyone else. She recognizes the danger to herself and others and she likely feels helpless to prevent it." Bren replied. Ana shook her head.

"No, I don't think she feels helpless. I don't think Hedy would ever feel helpless. She might be scared, she might feel she doesn't have much control over what is happening, but helpless isn't something I would say is part of her character. In any event, how about a walk, Mel?" Mel nodded and the two girls left Bren alone in the shop.

He stood in the shop, peering out the window, looking like someone in deep thought. He was alone; not even Maurice or Zelda were in the room. The temperature suddenly dropped and his breath was visible at his lips.

"It happens in threes. Another will join them." The voice of Adelaide whispered in Bren's ear, freezing the hairs along his neck. "Firewalker, are you the savior or the sinner?" He could practically feel the cold words.

"What do you want from me?" He managed to whisper. All his muscles seemed to be frozen and he stood rock still.

"There is danger for this house, for her, it swirls around this place, around you." Adelaide's voice trailed off, taking the cold with her. Bren rubbed his arms roughly and he looked to see if Hedy had returned but he was alone, with the words of a ghost.

CHAPTER TWELVE

Darro Raith was on Hedy's doorstep at the stroke of noon. Bren spotted him standing outside, rather than coming in, and he went to the door to investigate.

"I was waiting on a Miss Hedy Leckermaul. That's a mouthful, isn't it. Darro Raith, the gardener is calling." His Scottish accent was strong and Bren opened the door wide to invite the rather portly man into the house.

"Miss Leckermaul is in the shop, please do come in."

"If it is all the same to you, I'd prefer to stay outside. Me boots are muddled and I wouldna want to trample her lovely carpets." Darro instead walked to the wicker chair on the porch and gingerly sat down, testing if it would hold his weight.

"I'll let her know you are here." Bren closed the door and went back into the shop. Hedy was creating black rosettes for a cake ordered for a fortieth birthday party. She never understood the need to make forty seem like the mark of the grave; black roses were gorgeous anytime.

"Your gardener is here, he is on the porch. Darro Raith?" She looked up from the roses and Bren saw a smudge of black frosting had made its way to her temple. He picked up a napkin and said "May I?" before he carefully wiped it away.

"Oh good, I'm glad he is here. Thank you." She put down the piping bag and slipped out of the criss-cross apron. Today she was wearing a brown corduroy jumper and knee-high orange patent leather boots. Not exactly the right attire for stomping in the wet garden, but it would have to do.

"Mr. Raith. Thank you for coming." Hedy came out to the porch and Darro stood up, coming no higher than her shoulder. Hedy was tall but he was also quite short.

"My pleasure, Miss. I'm always keen for more work. I walked your garden when I arrived and we have work to do, haven't we? Overgrown, I'd say, with rascal weeds choking out everything. You have a foosty looking fir tree that will need to come out afore it topples into the house. That's a bit beyond my reach, I'm afraid." He chuckled as he headed down the stairs, leading Hedy toward the side yard to investigate the offending fir tree. Across the large yard, Mr. Jeffries was watching with interest.

Hedy followed Darro's quick pace as he pointed out the various sins of her garden, the invasive knotweed and sickly heirloom roses that would have to go. *Maybe Jeffries had been a little right about the garden*, she thought ruefully.

They finished their tour of the garden and headed back into the shop, with Hedy insisting that he come inside for a hot cup of coffee. "Since you're the customer, I canna say no." He trudged in the front door and found Bren in the shop, holding down the fort.

"Please sit down, Darro. Would you like a scone to go with your coffee?"

"Ah thank you, no. No offense, but you Americans don't know a proper scone. My grandmother, God rest her soul, would be a spinnin' in her Edinburgh grave in the kirkyard if she caught me eating one. But I wouldn't mind a bit of that cinnamon cake that looks so fetching."

Hedy cut him a large slice and brought it to the table. Bren shook his head when she offered him one as well. "Well, if you have your grandmother's recipe, I would love to give it a try." Darro gave her a look as if to say did he look like someone who would have a 100-year-old Scottish scone recipe, but said nothing as his mouth was too full of cinnamon cake.

"So, will you work on the garden for me?"

"Aye, I would be glad to. Nothing makes me happier than rustling about in the dirt, making everything good and fine. And as much as I find your cinnamon cake to my liking, I will need to charge you. My nightly weed don't come cheap." He smiled broadly at them but Bren looked confused at that.

"Bren, marijuana is legal here in Washington. I believe Darro is referring to that."

"Ah, thank you, now I see." Bren gave a small smile.

"You could use a puff or two, friend. You look as if your knickers were in a twist, pardon me saying." Darro winked at Bren with a smile, clearly meaning no offense.

"Well, with all the fires in town, I'd say everyone was on edge, wouldn't you?" Hedy said, watching a bit of cake settle into Darro's beard.

"Oh aye, nasty business, that. Me roommate is a fireman and he's been telling me about it. Dinna find no trace of either lady. Bad business indeed." The cake was gone and Darro rose to leave. "Is twenty dollars per hour acceptable to you? It might take me several full days to get her into shape but after that, it'll just be once a week until spring, and then we ramp up again. She'll be the Queen of the block a'fore I am done."

"Yes, that will be fine. Thank you, Darro." Hedy said and both she and Bren rose to say goodbye to the man.

"That's good to hear. I'll start in the morning, just after sun up. I like to get an early start at me work. Maybe Mr. Skinny Malinky Longlegs here can give me a hand." He winked again at Bren and Hedy burst out laughing.

"We will see you tomorrow, Darro, oh and take a cookie for your roommate. It is awful that the fires have been keeping him busy." Hedy took a large leaf cookie and put it in a cellophane bag. With a quick nod of the head, Darro Raith was gone.

"What a curious man, wouldn't you say?" Bren watched him scurry down the stairs and across the yard.

"He's charming, in a rumpled sort of way. I bet this is the first time someone has called you Skinny Malinky Longlegs."

"Yes, I would say that is true. Maybe I do need to try some of his nightly weed, he seems to enjoy it."

"Well, you can ask him about it tomorrow. I personally never touch the stuff. It has no effect on me whatsoever, which I find odd and also a bit disappointing, if I must say so." Hedy took Darro's dishes and headed back toward the kitchen. She had the black birthday cake to finish.

"Oh, I would say that is because you aren't like average people who need such things to escape the mundane. There is nothing about you that is mundane, Miss Leckermaul." She smiled at Bren and did her best imitation of a curtsy.

"I take that as a compliment, sir. The world needs more, not less, variety. How dull to be mundane."

"Hedy, I didn't mention it before but Adelaide paid me a visit while you were working in the kitchen earlier. She said there is danger for another." Hedy turned back to look at Bren, who was watching her with an expression that she couldn't read.

"How does she know that? I suppose she didn't

say. I wonder if all ghosts are so cryptic or if it is just Adelaide?" Hedy sounded exasperated.

"I don't know why she told me. Maybe she thought I could help somehow." From the clouded expression on his face, Hedy gathered that he might not be telling her everything that Adelaide had said. She hated feeling suspicious like this.

"Whatever we can do to help, we should do it. Just let me know if you have any ideas." Hedy turned back toward the counter, hoping her face didn't betray her doubts.

CHAPTER THIRTEEN

The girls had returned, hungry and ready for some tomato soup that had been simmering on the stove all morning. Bren had been waiting for them to come back.

"Do you have a computer in that backpack, Mel?" He asked simply.

Mel shook her head but she pulled out her smartphone. "I have Internet access on this, what are you looking for?"

"I'm not really sure, but I'm looking for a pattern of threes. Has there been a history of women or girls going missing in Enumclaw in sets of three?" Mel put down her soup spoon and entered her password.

"I can look online for reports of missing people from Enumclaw but honestly, I'm not sure all that information will be available. We would likely need access to police records or maybe to news articles at the library. I can show you where the library is located, if that helps." Mel pinched and swiped at the screen, entering a search for missing persons. She scrolled through the results.

"Why are you looking for this pattern, Bren?" Anahita asked in a flat voice.

"Something that Adelaide said while you were gone. She said it comes in threes. It occurred to me that there might be pattern to all this. I thought perhaps Mel could help me."

Anahita said nothing to this but Mel spoke up.

"From the looks of this list, there does seem to be periods with more missing people than others. Without really reviewing the data though, I couldn't say with certainty." Mel handed the phone to Bren and picked up her spoon again.

Bren scrolled the list, gathered by some unknown person for some unknown purpose.

"Alright, for example, according to this website, about two years ago, there was a murder of a woman, and a disappearance of two other women, all over the course of a month. Then nothing until now. Before that, about five years back, we see three hikers gone missing near Mount Enumclaw. Mel, would you be able to help me review all this data and make sense of it?" Mel nodded in response to his question.

"What are you all conspiring about?" Hedy lifted the cake platter up for them to see, showing off the gorgeously black cake with the perfect rosettes and chocolate spiderwebs. Hedy was rightfully proud of it; it was especially spectacular.

"Mel is going to help me do some research, I think I might have spotted a pattern to these disappearances. Can we borrow your car to go to the library?"

"Certainly. The key is hanging by the back door."

The front door bell rang, bringing customers into the shop and an end to their conversation. Mel finished her soup and gathered up her things to head to the library. Bren went upstairs to grab his jacket.

"I'm going with you, Mel." Ana reached over and gave Mel's arm a squeeze. "You know that there is something about Bren that bothers me. I don't trust him."

"Why would he offer to do this if he wasn't on the up and up?" Ana looked at her quizzically, and Mel rephrased her slang. "If he wasn't being honest?"

"What better way to throw suspicion off yourself than to look like you are helping. Remember, he was at the coffee stand before the fire. We don't know anything about him. For all we know, he could be setting these fires. Until I am sure about him, I am not letting you go anywhere without me." She squeezed Mel's arm again, keeping her hand resting against her skin.

"All set, Mel?" Bren had returned with his jacket and notebook, breaking the moment between them.

"Yes, we are ready." Anahita rose, still keeping her hand on Mel's arm. "Let's go to the library." If Bren was surprised that Anahita was also going, he didn't show it. The three of them headed toward the back door to get the car key.

Hedy kept busy while they were gone. The customer who had ordered the black birthday cake came by and was so impressed that she insisted on taking a photo of both the cake and Hedy so she could put it on Instagram, which Hedy knew nothing about. She herself would make a striking photo for Instagram, if she had been inclined to self-promotion. She really didn't understand the idea of social media and she didn't have a computer or smartphone anyway.

The house hadn't been dusted in a bit and Hedy took the opportunity of a lag in customers and the absence of travelers to do some tidying up. The entry tended to collect the most dust as it had the most unusual surfaces and objects. Almost all of her findings from her travels were kept in the entry hall, though she was quickly running out of room. Hedy was an avid collector and though she had inherited quite a few of her treasures from her mother and grandmother and previous generations of Leckermauls, some of the items she now dusted had been her own discoveries. The time she had spent in London, prowling the antique stalls on Portobello Road had yielded the rather disgusting looking monkey's paw in a glass box. The grim item had inspired W.W. Jacobs in 1902 to write his famous short story of the same name. She had considered donating it to a University for their literature department but the consensus was that the students would find far more disgust in the paw, than in the literary value. So, the paw stayed with Hedy. Her feather duster trailed along the glass edges and wood panels, with the task taking on a Zen like quality, soothing her. Everything she dusted had a story, they had a piece of memory for her; mostly they were good memories but there were a few bitter ones as well. Just seeing the objects though, brought her back to where she was and who she was with for everyone one of them. It was a homecoming.

* * *

The threesome, back from the library caught her in her thoughts. "Any luck?" she asked as they filed into the shop and gathered back around Mel's favorite table.

"Well, yes and no. We found evidence that this town has had its share of strange disappearances, typically in groupings of three, but I don't know that we learned much that would help identify who is behind it." Bren spoke, looking at Mel and Anahita, who both nodded in agreement.

Mel pulled out a sheet of notebook paper as she said, "We went back to the 1920s, and found Adelaide's murder in this house was actually one of three that summer. All three girls were strangled with a necklace and their bodies left in their homes. The police never arrested the killer but they had several suspects. After the three murders, there wasn't another pattern until into the

1930s - that time it was three people who went missing and were never found. The late 40s had another trio of deaths, then there was a lull until 1965, when three people survived an arsonist who tried to burn down their house." Mel reviewed her notes as she spoke.

"Was anyone caught in all that time?" Hedy placed a plate of beetle shaped cookies on the table; they were tinted a strange shade of dark iridescent green, much like a real figeater beetle.

"The 1965 case led to a conviction. It was an old man, who had lived in the town all his life. George J. Wilkenson was his name. He had actually been a suspect in the murders in the 1920s but there was no evidence to tie him to the crimes. He died in prison in the early 70s." Mel finished speaking before she bit the head off on of the cookies. They were cardamom flavored, without a hint of bug flavor, or so Mel hoped.

"So, nothing you found really sheds any light on what is happening now?" Hedy didn't know what she had expected but she was disappointed nonetheless.

"The pattern picked up again in the 1990s. Again, always girls or women, usually missing and never found. The newspapers at the time attributed those who went missing as victims of the Green River Killer, who wasn't caught until 2001. Not all the missing were from Enumclaw, some were from other close areas like Buckley or Black Diamond, but they all seem to occur with a few weeks of each other." Mel took another big bite of her cookie and offered the plate to Ana, who shook her head politely. She took another from the plate. Sleuthing appeared to have energized Mel's appetite.

"Fast forward and things had been quiet for years and then it started up again five years ago. The police have made no arrests." Mel finished another bite of beetle.

Anahita piped up for the first time. "If the same person is doing this as the one from the 1990s, then the odds are this person is older. But from what we found, the pattern is different. The fires and missing victims now do not match the events from the 90s or even the last group of missing campers from five years ago. The only things they have in common is the grouping of three. It doesn't look like the current fires are connected." She looked quickly at Bren and then back toward Mel.

"We did find out something useful while we were at the library. There was a sign posted that there is going to be a community meeting at city hall tonight to discuss the fires and what is being done." Mel said.

The front door bell tinkled and Hedy rose from the table to greet the customer. "I think we should go. If nothing else, maybe the officials will have some good news about the missing people." The others nodded in agreement and Hedy popped back behind the counter to box up some blackbird pies.

* * *

The City Hall Council chamber was filled to capacity, a raucous noise bouncing around the walls as everyone speculated on the source of the fires. Hedy had found spots for them in the crowd near the back wall. Behind them, unnoticed, Lyssa had also slipped into the crowd.

"If I could have your attention please, thank you." The police chief waved his arms and tried to quiet down the crowd. Slowly the voices trickled down to silence.

"The purpose of tonight's meeting is to let you know where things stand with the two fires that happened this week, and to ask you all to be vigilant and report anything you see that looks suspicious. At this time, we do not have a suspect for the fires, both of which have been ruled as arson." The crowd murmured, with several voices heard to say "I knew it".

"What about Gretchen? What are you doing about finding her and Shannon?" The voice that called out was Gretchen's mother, who was seated near the front of the room. Hedy heard the rapid fire clicking of a camera near her; the Courier-Herald had a reporter there to capture the event.

"We are doing everything we can to find the missing women and we are working with the FBI. At this time, we have no evidence of kidnapping or foul play. The missing women are simply that, missing - we don't know if they left on their own accord or were taken." The crowd did not like that comment and their voices rose in unison. Chief Dixon raised his hands again for quiet.

"But at this time, we are treating this like a kidnapping situation for both Shannon and Gretchen. We are asking anyone with information to come forward, no matter how small it might seem. We currently have no suspects identified."

"Have you talked with those weirdos that live on the commune, over by Buckley? Socialist freaks, all of them." A man in the front row, wearing a tee-shirt with a large US flag on the back, shouted toward the Chief. The crowd erupted.

"Let's keep this civil, alright. We are talking to anyone who might be of interest in either of these cases."

A woman shouted from the crowd, "I'm sorry the gals are missing, but good riddance to both of those places, eyesores in my opinion. Who needs a coffee stand with girls in bikinis? It's not decent. And that yoga place, practicing some heathen religion in there."

"Hey, shut up, OK? Why do you think it is OK to say crap like that?" A young woman shouted from the back of room. She was standing next to Lyssa, who had just slipped away from the room.

"Nobody asked you anything, so you shut up." Flag man stood up and shouted back toward her. The crowd began to get loud again, with people taking up sides.

"People, enough. There is no point going on like this. Let's quit pointing fingers and..." The Chief's words were drowned out by the crowd noise.

"This town used to be family friendly until people like you moved in." The man pointed back toward the woman, wagging his finger in the air. "Why don't you move back to Seattle or wherever the hell you come from. We don't want your kind here."

"My kind? You mean someone who doesn't breathe through their mouth or drag their knuckles like you? Fuck off, man."

"Aren't you a classy lady. Nice mouth on you. Someone ought to teach you a lesson." Flag man nearly spat as he spoke, snapping the back of his hand in the air.

"Hey jerk, that's enough. You take a swing at her, you will deal with me." A man a few seats away from the woman stood up and started to press toward Flag man. The crowd could sense a fight was coming and it started to egg them on. Things were getting ugly and out of hand.

"Come on, we should go." Hedy tried to push toward the door but people were blocking the way.

"Oh, I'll deal with you, junior. Me and my Smith & Wesson." Half the crowd laughed and the other half gave a sharp gasp.

"Enough!" The Chief had reached Flag man and he bellowed out to the crowd. "This meeting is over. Everybody out. We have enough going on without everyone acting up. Tempers are high so go home and cool off, and remember what I said about reporting anything suspicious."

Hedy and the group made their way slowly toward the exit, shuffling behind some people who were visibly disappointed that the fight had been prevented. Everyone poured out of the building into the chilly night air. Pockets of people were scattered on the sidewalk and as the group walked, they heard various phrases of "shoulda smacked that bitch" or "redneck asshole" depending on which side of the debate they were on. All along the path toward the car, there were trees with crows perched, as if they were watching the people below. There must have been two dozen of them watching with keen attention.

"Let's get out of here." Mel took Ana by the hand and they hurriedly walked toward the car, with Bren keeping to the rear, just in case anyone started something behind them. A cacophony of caws filled the cold air.

"Is this town always like this, Mel?" Ana slid into the backseat with Mel as Hedy fired up the Corvair.

"No, I've never seen it like this. Sure, there are people who are really conservative and then you have people moving in who come from more liberal places, but the most you ever see are yard signs during elections getting vandalized, or maybe you hear about a bar fight if someone does something stupid. I've never seen people just go at it like that in public, like it is OK to say those things."

"Some of it is the times we live in, and some of it is the fear from the fires, but there is also something else, something new." Hedy was watching the road but seeing the angry face of the Flag man in her vision as she drove.

"Well, it's not like we just met the goddess of rage and madness, right?" said Ana and they all understood. It did feel like some kind of madness had settled on to people.

"I'm not quite ready to believe in a legendary goddess yet, because it is too unbelievable to consider, but it certainly does seem like people have lost their damn minds." Mel pulled her sweater around herself tightly.

"Mel, to paraphrase a famous quote, things are real whether you believe in them or not. What do you think Maurice would say to that?" Hedy chuckled as she thought of Mel's recent conversation with the chinchilla. "Strange things are happening all the time whether you know about them or not."

The Corvair pulled into the driveway and Hedy knew immediately that something was very wrong. The front door was wide open, with light spilling out onto the front porch.

"Mel, Anahita, you stay in the car." Hedy jumped out and headed up to the porch, with Bren right behind her.

Hedy was inside the entry before Bren could stop her. The hallway had smashed glass running from one end to the other. The damage was haphazard, with some items left alone and others seemingly smashed to pieces.

"I'll check the shop and the kitchen." Bren darted into the shop but almost immediately called out, "Everything looks fine." Hedy was crouching in front of the remnants of the monkey's paw, torn in half like it was a piece of paper. The tall glass curio cabinet had been toppled over and the contents scattered all over the carpet. The glass shelves appeared to have been smashed with the axe head that once belonging to Lizzie Borden lying next to the shards on the carpet.

Bren returned from the kitchen. "Nothing is moved. What about upstairs?" They both glanced at the thicket gate at the foot of the stairs, still in place.

"No, whoever did this was looking for something here in the hallway. I would guess they didn't find it because nothing looks missing, just smashed up."

"Any ideas what that might have been?" Bren helped Hedy as she stood up and walked back toward the porch. She waved to Mel and Anahita to signal the all-clear.

"No. If they wanted something valuable, there were several rare pieces they left untouched. If they wanted to just smash, why would they have selected some things and not hit everything? I don't know but I'm guessing it has something to do with Lyssa."

Mel and Anahita came up the stairs and peered into the entry, gasping at the damage. Hedy came back inside and slipped out of her jacket. It would be a long night cleaning up this mess.

"Bren, will you do me a favor and drive Mel home? I don't want her walking this late. Anahita, if you'll go along and keep her company, that would be nice. I'm going to look for Zelda or Maurice to see if they saw anything."

"I'd rather not leave you alone. Why don't you come with us and we will help you clean up when we get back." Bren said as he took the car keys from Hedy's hand.

"I'd rather start straightening up my house, if you don't mind. Plus, I might cry a little for the things destroyed and I'd rather do that on my own. Thanks, though." She gave Bren's hand a squeeze and she watched them leave the porch toward the car. She closed the door and leaned heavily against it.

"What the hell is happening around here?" She said to no one in particular, though in this house, she might have received an answer from several inhabitants. But the ghost, the cat and the chinchilla were nowhere to be seen.

Hedy walked toward the kitchen to get the broom and look for the menagerie. She had no doubt they were safe; she was sure that whoever had done this wasn't interested in them.

"Alice, have you seen Zelda or Maurice? We've had an intruder." Alice was on her perch, looking for all the world unaware of the ruckus.

"I just came in, Hedy. The house has been quiet and I haven't seen hide nor hair of either Zelda or Maurice. I assumed they were upstairs or somewhere about." The magpie looked as startled as one could look with no eyebrows.

"I hope they are upstairs, maybe even sleeping through all this. Someone came in and smashed up the entry, there is glass everywhere." Hedy grabbed the broom and dustpan from the wall hook, along with several paper sacks from the grocery store.

"Oh Hedy, I am so sorry to hear it. I would help you but not much I can do with these." Alice flapped her wings as if to shrug.

"That's alright, Alice. You can do me a favor though and go upstairs and look for the other two? Let them know there is glass all over and to tread carefully." Alice nodded and she took off from her perch.

Back in the entry, Hedy began lightly sweeping the large pieces of glass into a pile so she could carefully place them into the bags. She hadn't lied when she said she might cry; tears came quickly to her eyes as she saw her treasures smashed amongst the shards.

"What were you looking for?" Hedy muttered, wiping her eye with her sleeve to avoid touching her face in case she had any glass on her fingertips. Almost all the pieces in her collection were there in the hall. She had a few items tucked away in a chest on the third floor, and one or two large items boxed up in the garage. She tried to take a quick mental inventory as to what might have been out of sight of the intruder.

"There are the Houdini items from auction," Hedy murmured. They were the handcuffs and leg irons from the Chinese water torture trick, and she had them boxed up in the garage. She had picked those up in London at an auction in 2013.

"There is the taxidermy Dali octopus." Another auction acquisition, it was the dead octopus that Dali had used to paint part of *Triumph of the Sea.* She had a print of the work on the wall in the entry but the octopus was a bit too worn to display. No one would want to steal that.

"Oh, the box from Crete." Hedy stopped mid-sweep as she remembered the wooden box she had brought back from her summer in Crete several years ago. The box itself was nothing special - it actually had been used to store jars of olives, but the contents were some artifacts from all over Greece.

"What happened here?" Both Zelda and Maurice had squeezed through the thicket gate and were standing far away from the mayhem on the last stair step.

"You didn't hear anything?" They each shook their heads.

"I was out in the yard, doing a bit of vole hunting, and Maurice was up dozing on the windowsill by the library. He's practically deaf anyway." Zelda gave Maurice an accusatory look, as if he could have prevented the destruction around them.

"Well, someone was looking for something and it seems they wanted to smash things up in the process. You two better stay clear of here until I get all this glass cleaned up."

"Well, at least they didn't smash the Winchester spiderweb, that is my favorite." Maurice said and Hedy had been relieved to see that as well.

"But since they tore up the monkey's paw, do you mind if I have it?" Zelda had already spied the two halves of the paw, stuffing sprouting from both sides.

"Perhaps a proper burial would be better, Zelda. As fond as I am of the story, I think the paw itself has been through enough trauma before becoming a cat's plaything." Zelda sniffed slightly but didn't press the issue. Clearly now was not the time to get snippy with Hedy. Besides, she could always dig it up later.

"What do you think the intruder wanted, Hedy?" Maurice stayed perched on the step to avoid any glass shards. His face was a mask of unsaid "I told you so".

"I don't know, Maurice. Whatever it was, I don't think they found it."

"Yet" said the chinchilla and he squeezed back through the bramble gate to the safety of the stairs.

CHAPTER FOURTEEN

Bren and Ana returned to find the entry in much better shape than when they left. The broken glass was gone and the curio cabinet was upright, if still broken and empty. The artifacts were gathered up and sitting on two of the tables in the shop. Hedy herself was sitting at Mel's table with a wooden box in front of her.

"Thank you for taking Mel home. I must apologize for how your stay has been going. I really have never had such an experience but nonetheless, as your host, I feel responsible." Ana and Bren both shook their heads.

"Nonsense, Hedy. None of this is your fault. We can handle what is happening." Bren came over and gave her a small pat on the shoulder.

"What's in the box?" Ana sat down across from her, watching as Hedy began to pry open the top of the crate with a small bar.

"I can't be certain but it might be what the intruder was looking for." Hedy used the edge of the bar to lift the nailed edge of the lid. The slight scent of olives wafted out.

Inside the box was a nest of shaved and coiled wood, cushioning the objects inside. Hedy took out a tiny figurine, wrapped in lengths of linen. She unwrapped it to show a pale white figure of a Minoan snake goddess, no bigger than her thumb. She placed it carefully on the pile of beige linen. Next to it in the box was a single arrowhead, obviously very old; it looked like it was bronze with a dull green patina and four sharp looking edges to it. She carefully took it out and also placed it on the linen. The last item was a small terracotta bottle, which was missing its stopper.

"What is all that?" Bren carefully picked up the arrowhead, twirling it slowly in his fingers.

"A few items that I bought off a peddler in Crete. He claimed they were rare pieces but given the low price, I had my doubts. He had some wild stories about the items, which is why I bought them. The most valuable thing would probably be the snake goddess figure. The terracotta bottle is a perfume bottle, and then there is the old arrowhead." Ana picked up the terracotta bottle and gave a slight sniff.

"Marjoram." Ana looked amazed that something that old could still have a bit of fragrance. "What were the stories?"

"As I recall, the snake goddess figure came from the palace of King Minos, of the Minotaur fame. The bottle supposedly belonged to the Oracle of Delphi, and the arrowhead was found near the summit of Mount Olympus. The storyteller was so entertaining, I bought the items on a whim. Not my best purchase, to be sure. There may have been more than a few glasses of ouzo involved."

"Why would the intruder want any of these? I mean, not to be rude, but you have far nicer things in your collection than these items." Bren put the arrowhead back on the linen. He didn't like the way it felt in his hand.

"Oh, I agree. I had these stored in my room upstairs because they aren't that appealing, frankly, and because I'm limited on space. But if the intruder didn't find what they were looking for in the entry, these are one of the few things that I didn't have on display."

"I assume we are operating under the theory that this was Lyssa, yes?" Ana placed the terracotta bottle down and picked up the little snake goddess. Something so tiny had amazing detail. She ran her thumb along the smooth alabaster surface.

"I don't know who else it might have been." Hedy gathered up the arrowhead and nestled it back into the wood shavings. Ana handed her back the figurine to wrap in linen.

"Well, if indeed Lyssa is who we think she is, then I suppose it makes sense she is after a Greek artifact. But I really can't see what these trinkets would mean to her." Ana placed the perfume bottle into the wood and Hedy placed the lid back on the box.

"Until we know the answer to that question, I think we better keep this box under lock and key." Hedy said.

"What about hiding it in the old fruit cellar? I found the door when I was raking and you could stash it away down there and no one would be the wiser. We can keep an eye on it there." Bren offered. Hedy had forgotten she even had a fruit cellar; it was the last place she would think to store anything of value.

"That sounds like a good idea. Tomorrow, I'll brave the spiders and find a good spot for this. For tonight, I'll keep it under my bed." Hedy stood up, exhausted suddenly. It had been a long stressful day and all she wanted to do was crawl into her bed and sleep.

"I am going to retire for the night. It's been a rather tiring day." She gave them both a weak smile and picked up the box.

"Sleep well, Hedy." Ana gave her a smile as Hedy walked slowly toward the entry, and she gave them both a small wave as she turned the corner.

"Bren, we need to talk." Ana said firmly.

CHAPTER FIFTEEN

"What's on your mind, Anahita?" He sounded polite but not overly friendly. They hadn't exactly hit it off in their short time in Hedy's house.

"I know about Seattle." Anahita tried to meet his gaze without wavering. She didn't like confrontation.

"What about Seattle?" Bren looked genuinely confused.

"You said you sailed in to Seattle, and you came in on a cargo boat from China, yes? Your boat landed early last week, but you've only been here since Monday." Ana's voice had the slightest accusatory edge to it.

"How do you know that? Seattle has boats coming in and out of the port all the time?" Bren's irritation was beginning to show.

"Not the *Liu Lin*, the ship you came in on. I found the paperwork in your room."

"You went through my things? What gave you the right?" Bren's face darkened and his voice was low and angry.

"When fires mysteriously strike a town where a salamander has just appeared, etiquette goes out the window. My apologies but I had to know who I was dealing with here." Ana's gaze and voice were neutral, without a hint of escalation.

"The day after the *Liu Lin* arrives, there is a fire in Seattle. Unexplained, it destroyed a house on Queen Anne hill that happened to be a waystation. You were there, weren't you?"

"No. I wasn't there, Anahita. There are two way-stations in Seattle - one on Queen Anne hill, the other over in West Seattle. I stayed there because there wasn't any room in the one on Queen Anne."

Anahita said nothing. It was a minute or two before either of them spoke. The fact that the Concierge would have Bren's itinerary at their fingertips wasn't spoken by either of them.

"Look, I know how it looks and I understand why you are concerned about me. If, suddenly, people were drowning, pulled under the water, I might think you were involved somehow. But just because I am a salamander, that doesn't mean I am involved in these fires, or the one in Seattle."

Anahita paused again before she spoke. She was clearly parsing her words in her head.

"Perhaps that is true, Bren. But you were involved in the fire in Los Angeles, the one that killed your wife."

All the air left the room it seemed as Bren looked at Anahita with astonishment. He opened his mouth several times before speaking.

"How do you know about that?" His voice was low and stained with pain.

"You don't use the computer that much, I know, but there isn't much that goes on that isn't captured somewhere on the Internet. I found the newspaper story about the fire in Laurel Canyon. Luckily, it was quickly put out by the firefighters, but not before it had destroyed the homes of three families, including the Aldebrands. Lily Aldebrand was the only casualty."

"Yes, my home burned down, and yes, my wife died. It was an accident." Bren's words cut through the silence.

"Bren, the newspaper said it was an unexplained fire, no accelerant found, no cause known. They didn't rule out arson. What caused the fire?"

Bren said nothing, he stood up and walked toward the doorway as if to leave Anahita and the whole conversation behind him. He turned and looked back over his shoulder.

"I was younger, unable to control my fire as I can now. Lily and I had only been married a short while, and I was madly in love with her. So madly in love that I didn't see the signs that she was cheating on me. I came home one night and found the letters, the letters from her lover and her plans to run away with him. I was furious, angrier than I have ever been in my life. Lily laughed when I confronted her. She laughed at being caught... at me." Bren swallowed and looked ashen, the memory of that night clear on his face.

"I don't remember what happened after that. Only the heat, the anger, the fire around me. I know I walked out of the house but I don't know anything more than that. I found myself in my car down the road and the flames were lighting up the sky."

Ana tried to speak but he held up his hand to silence her.

"I have to live with the things I have done, Anahita. I have to live with the knowledge that a human being that I loved died because of me. It's what sent me on my mission to find a cure for what I am. I live with this pain, but I swear to you I had nothing to do with these fires. You can believe me or not, you can tell Hedy if you want to, but my past is not going to chase me from my future." Bren walked out of the doorway, leaving Anahita alone with her accusations.

Ana went to her room, exhausted both in body and mind. It had been an awful day, and in truth, an awful week. She ran the bath water and added a few drops from the vial around her neck. The water was cool, far cooler than most people would find comfortable, but to an undine like Ana, it was perfect.

She slipped into the water and let herself sink to the bottom of the tub, submerging her head and feeling her hair float around her. She opened her eyes and felt the cool water against her lashes. Every pore on her body opened up and breathed in the water. It was if she had been wearing a tight corset and now, she could finally take a deep breath.

Ana stayed submerged for several minutes, floating and letting the water wash away the strain and fear from the day. It seemed like she had left Iran and been finding herself in trouble ever since. Her mother had warned her not to leave, to stay and live her life there among her people, but Ana knew her life was not there. Not in modern Iran, and not with her family. She loved them, beyond words, but she couldn't be herself with them. Even in a family of undines, there could be things that wouldn't be accepted.

And so, she had left Iran. She knew the United States was where she wanted to travel first, though ever since she had landed in Miami and made her way west, she had questioned that decision. Perhaps Scotland would have been a better choice, a place with many lakes and rivers and wild spaces. But America had called to her and she was making her way to Alaska.

Ana finally came up from the water and took a long quiet breath. Her skin felt alive and her mind quiet, for the first time in several days. She soaked in the tepid water and let her fingers trail through the water, back and forth as she traced the birthmark just below her navel. The small inverted triangular shape with a small wavy line crossing at the point. The mark of the undine, showing both her true nature and her longevity. Undines could live for centuries, but only if they never fell in love. Those who met their mate found their souls and their mortality. As was the case so often with love, such stories held danger and sacrifice for both.

"Mel..." Ana said her name and thought about the girl who had come to mean so much to her in such a short time. By now, she should be moving along to her next waystation in Canada but she couldn't leave yet. She wanted to stay to make sure Mel was safe and because she couldn't quite bring herself to go just yet.

Mel's name was on her lips as she drifted off to sleep in the tub, unafraid of slipping beneath the water as she slept. Tomorrow would bring more trouble no doubt, but it would also bring Mel, and that was enough to make it worthwhile.

* * *

The dawn came behind dark gray clouds, barely bringing the morning light into the house of Griffin Avenue. Hedy normally woke when the light pierced her window but today, she overslept and woke to the gray. The house seemed colder, with drafts coming in from the corners and the edges that naturally had buckled a bit over a hundred years. She wrapped herself in a thick robe and went downstairs to stoke up the potbelly stove and light the fireplaces in the living room and parlor.

Out the front window, almost part of the gray landscape, she saw a figure moving in her garden and for a moment, she forgot about Darro, the gardener. She squinted against the glass and could make out his squat frame as he wrestled with an unruly juniper bush. She'd make him a pot of hot chocolate and bring it out to the front porch, once she has the fires stoked.

"It is freezing this morning, Hedy." Alice was trilling from her perch in the kitchen and Hedy detected a slight chatter in her voice.

"Yes, it certainly is. It seems to have taken a chill overnight. Yesterday was so lovely and I hardly needed a sweater. Today feels chilly to the bone. I'm stoking up the stove right now." The magpie clucked in appreciation and hopped from her perch to the edge of the counter closest to the stove.

"The cold has just seemed to settle over the house like some kind of blanket. I flew out this morning for a quick jaunt, and I swear, once I left the neighborhood, it was warmer and less gray." Alice raised and lowered her wings, fanning the warmth closer to her body.

"Well, that doesn't surprise me. Weather around here is so changeable. We might be getting a bit of wind from the north, bringing in some cold air. It's a good day for hot soup and pots of tea."

"Someone better chip the ice off Maurice, he fell asleep near the window in the parlor and I'll just bet he's near frozen." Zelda said as she came in from whatever corner she had spent the night. Hedy chuckled and walked back into the shop to find that Maurice had indeed fallen asleep on the windowsill. No ice to be seen but as Hedy picked him up, his fur was decidedly chilly.

"What's this? What's happening?" Maurice started as she picked him up and carried him back to the warmth of the kitchen.

"It's chilly this morning, Maurice. I thought you might appreciate the warmth of the stove. Sorry to disturb you." She placed him gently on the chair near the stove and he settled into the cushion.

"Thank you, Hedy. Not sure what came over me, I just was so sleepy last night I couldn't make it up the stairs."

"Old age will do that to you, Maurice." Zelda licked her paws gently.

"I think everyone was tired last night, Zelda. I barely made it to my own bed before collapsing. Give Maurice a break today, eh?" Hedy took a copper saucepan from the cupboard and filled it with milk to simmer on the stove. In a small bowl, she mixed the dark cocoa powder, sugar, and a pinch of salt and cardamom.

"Cocoa? Oh yes please." Maurice perked up at the thought of a saucer of cocoa.

"Certainly. It is a cocoa kind of morning. I do have a favor to ask of you all though." The menagerie perked up as Hedy hardly ever asked them for anything. "Today, will you keep a watchful eye on the house? After the break in last night, I am worried that the intruder might try to come back. The more eyes we have on the house, the better. In fact, if that fox is still around, maybe he would be willing to be on watch as well. It doesn't hurt to ask."

"As if you could trust a fox. Everyone knows they are liars and thieves." Maurice spat his disgust at the thought. Chinchillas and foxes had a long history of hatred.

"Allegiance can be bought, Maurice, especially with foxes. I suspect a meat pie would keep the rascal allied with us." Zelda had her own suspicions of foxes, though not to the degree of Maurice. Maurice's own brother had been eaten by one.

"It was just a thought. But in any event, if you all can be vigilant and help me keep an eye on things today, I would appreciate it." The milk began to bubble and Hedy whisked in the cocoa mixture, careful to keep the milk from scorching.

"Of course, Hedy. We'll be on guard for you. I'll spread the word to my circle, nothing like a few eyes in the sky keeping watch. Well, everyone but those crows. I don't trust them." Alice chirped, hopping a bit now that she was warm and had a job to do.

"Yes, nothing like those keen intellects, the birds, to be able to spot trouble from the sky." Zelda said softly, almost under her breath, though Hedy heard her and gave her a disapproving look. Alice didn't seem to catch the sarcasm.

"Indeed, the more the merrier, eh Zelda?" The

magpie hopped back to her perch.

CHAPTER SIXTEEN

"Good day, Miss Hedy. I'm fair puckled from wrestling with that juniper! I'm not the youngin' I once was." Darro came up the stairs, slipping off the leather gloves he had on so he could accept the mug of cocoa. It felt raw and bleak out to Hedy, but Darro seemed oblivious in his short sleeve shirt.

"Wouldn't you rather come in to drink your cocoa? It will freeze up on you out here."

"Oh no, I'm fine here. I wouldna want to track up your carpet and I'll finish this off in a flash."

"What's your plan for the day, Darro?" Hedy hugged her robe a bit more around her to keep out the chill.

"Now that the juniper is out, dastardly thing, I am going to move on to that dead tree we talked about. It's near your neighbor's fence so I will need to talk with him about it. After that, I'll be pulling some blighted rosebushes and taking the clippers to your hedges to give 'em a good whackin'. I'll be at it all morning." Darro took another big drink from the mug, finishing the cocoa in record time. He smacked his lips in satisfaction and handed the mug back to Hedy.

"Thank ye kindly. I'll be back at it now, before me knees have a chance to complain." With that, he was back down the stairs, dragging the offending juniper bush toward his pickup truck. Hedy gratefully took the mug back into the warmth of the house.

"It's a cold day, isn't it?" Ana had come downstairs, her dark hair braided and coiled on top of her head, for the first time not flowing freely around her.

"It certainly is. I have hot cocoa in the kitchen on the stove if you'd like some. I am going to pop upstairs to get dressed so I can get the store ready to open. Feel free to help yourself to whatever you'd like to eat."

Hedy shuffled back up the stairway and into the chill of the third floor. She found a long argyle sweater dress in the back of her wardrobe and she hurriedly slipped it on, finding a pair of long socks and boots to shield her feet. It was too chilly at her dressing table to fuss with her normal hairstyle, so she tied it all back in high ponytail and finished if off with a mustard yellow bow. She gave herself a quick look in the mirror and then hurriedly made the bed so she could get back to the warmth downstairs. She was so distracted by the cold that she almost forgot to grab the box she had stashed under the dust ruffle. She didn't relish the thought of heading into the dank and dark fruit cellar, but it probably was the best place to hide the box.

Hedy rejoined Ana in the kitchen, where the girl was sipping on cocoa and eating a bit of left-over salmon from the refrigerator. Hedy couldn't think of a less appetizing combination but she said nothing to Ana. The menagerie had left the warmth of the kitchen, taking their duties to patrol the house seriously. Hedy began mashing up bananas for some bread she was going to make for the day.

"I would have thought Mel would have been here by now," Hedy said as she looked over toward Ana as she mashed the bananas.

"She has a test this morning, so we won't see her until later this afternoon." Ana said with resignation. Her disappointment was palpable.

"You two have really hit it off, haven't you?" Hedy remarked.

"Mel is a special person." Ana's voice was soft and neutral.

"Does she know?" Hedy didn't quite know how to ask such a question, and truthfully it really wasn't her place to ask, but she felt protective toward Mel for some reason.

Ana paused for a bit too long before she spoke quietly, "No".

"Do you plan to tell her?"

Again, there was a long pause before Ana spoke. "About me being an undine? Honestly, I don't know. It feels dishonest not to say something but if I am leaving town in a few days, why burden her with the knowledge?"

"That's not what I meant. I meant, do you plan to tell her that you like her." Hedy carefully kept her eyes on the bowl of banana mash in front of her, trying not to make Ana more uncomfortable than she likely already was.

"I guess that depends. It depends on whether I plan to stay around or not. Right now, I'm scheduled to be in Vancouver, BC in a few days. Again, why burden her with my feelings if I am just leaving town?"

"I don't think telling someone how you feel is a burden. Even if you are leaving, it seems right to let her know that you care about her. Goodness knows there isn't enough care in this world, we have to grab on to every little scrap that comes our way. This is just my unsolicited opinion, and you can tell me I am all wet if you want, but if it were me, I would tell her - tell her everything. She's young, but then so are you, and nothing seems insurmountable when you are young." Hedy finished her advice and started adding allspice and nutmeg to the bowl.

"I'll think about it. I have a lot of thinking to do actually. Telling Mel isn't as simple as you might think. There is a risk for us both."

"The risk that she might like you as well? That's hardly a large risk. I think that is fairly obvious, at least to me."

Ana had wondered if she was crazy to think that

maybe Mel liked her too, but now Hedy had confirmed it. That just made her decision all the more difficult.

"No, it is more than that. There is danger, real danger for one who loves an undine." Hedy stopped mixing and turned to face Ana. She looked concerned for the first time.

"I don't know how much you know about us, but we aren't like other elementals, like Bren for example. Bren has his gifts but in other ways, he is much like a human. He lives and dies as humans do. Undines are different. We are born without souls and because we don't have souls, we live a very long time - hundreds of years.

"But if a human and an undine fall in love, that love changes us. We become more human, we lose our longevity and we in essence gain a soul from that love. We would live and grow old and die, just like everyone else."

"That doesn't sound very dangerous, as long as you wish to live a mortal life as a human." Hedy couldn't understand the concern.

"The danger is that if the human is unfaithful to the undine, that connection, that soul that unites them, it severs and the human will die. How can I ask anyone to risk that?" Ana couldn't imagine asking anyone to face such a fate just to love her.

"But you assume that the human would be unfaithful. Yes, love doesn't always last, but there is a difference between falling out of love and being unfaithful. If you find the one that truly loves you, what risk is there to either of you? Being unfaithful means they never really loved that person, that there was only lust, or need, or some other emotion behind it all. True love, the kind that can give an undine a soul, how could such a thing ever be mistaken for some other emotion?

"My advice to you is still the same. I would be honest with Mel and tell her everything. You've only known her a few days and there is nothing to rush into or any big decisions to make. But start your friendship honestly and you can't go wrong from there. At least that is what I think. Take it for what it is worth." Hedy returned to her bowl, hoping that she hadn't overstepped her bounds with Ana; the young woman was hard to read. She had made her fair share of mistakes over the years and she only wanted to help someone else avoid them, if she could.

Ana brought her empty cup to the sink and gave Hedy a small hug. "Thank you. I'll think about what you said. Maybe I'll take a walk and wait for Mel to finish her test. I do my best thinking outside." Ana left the room and she felt lighter in her heart than she had in some time.

CHAPTER SEVENTEEN

The ruckus started outside before the banana bread was even out of the oven. Hedy could hear Darro's voice all the way in the kitchen, though she couldn't make out the words. She found herself at the front door just as Bren was coming down the stairs.

"What's happening?" Bren had sprinted down from his bedroom, pulling on his shoe as he took the last step.

"Not sure, I just hear Darro yelling about something." Hedy opened the front door and the volume of the noise doubled. Both Darro and Mr. Jeffries were in a full-throated yelling match.

"You just ripped out my rose bushes! Those are my property!" Jeffries was screaming from the sidewalk, shaking his fist at Darro, who still had one of the rose bushes in his hand.

"You're off your head, old man! Those bushes are on this side of your fence. They have nothing to do with you!" Darro gave the bush a shake for good measure.

"The fence isn't the property line, you oaf. I actually own three feet to the west of the fence, which is exactly where those bushes were planted. Those bushes have been there for fifteen years!"

"You are daft! What makes you think the property on the other side of the damn fence belongs to you? Why the hell would there be a fence that wasn't on the line? And they are just a couple of natty old rose bushes, covered in fungus and blight." Darro roared again, giving the bush a toss into the back of his truck. Hedy and Bren reached the pair and narrowly avoided a face full of thorns.

"Hold on, what is this all about? What's with all the shouting?" Hedy looked from one red face to the other.

"This man has stolen my property. He removed those rose bushes, and they are mine. You've no right to take my property." Mr. Jeffries nearly spat at Hedy as he spoke.

"Mr. Jeffries, those are not your rose bushes. They are on my side of the property line. You can see the fence quite clearly..."

"As I told this imbecile, that fence doesn't mark the property. The previous owner of your house put it up twelve years ago, when I wasn't living at home. I left it up because she was an old woman and didn't have the means to take it down and build a new one in the proper place. I certainly wasn't going to pay for a new fence, so I left it alone. But those are my bushes!"

"If your property laws are anything like California, it's adverse possession; I hate to tell you this but by leaving the fence in place for all these years, you've given the land to Ms. Leckermaul." Bren tried to keep the smile out of his voice but he didn't do a very good job.

"What the hell are you talking about?" Jeffries eyed the thin man with contempt.

"By failing to claim back the land, you have relinquished your right to it. You've lost those three feet due to being too cheap to replace the fence. Those rose bushes and every other plant along that fence belongs to her."

Jeffries let out a roar of disbelief and frustration. "You are a liar! You and that white-haired whore." Bren started to make a move toward Jeffries, but Hedy stopped him.

"Come on, both of you. He's obviously unbalanced. Mr. Jeffries, if you come on to my property again, I will call the police. You are not welcome. Come on, Darro, Bren, let's go." The three of them left the old man shaking with rage on the sidewalk.

"You'll hear from my lawyer. This isn't over!"

"Ah, go boil your head, you old git." Darro called back over his shoulder. "I have some more roses to rip up."

* * *

True to her word, Anahita had indeed walked to

wait for Mel to finish her test at the high school. She had taken her time, strolling the streets, with the tidy bungalows and turn of the 20th century two story houses. The yards were large and full of the remnants of summer. Ana admired the sprawling lawns, the fields of green that you would never see in her part of Iran. Lawns seemed like such an American ideal - a large patch of green that required maintenance, money and time to keep up, but often was only enjoyed through the front window or driving by. It was rare to see families out on their lawns, at least in Ana's experience so far. It was something they kept up rather than enjoyed. She wondered why.

The high school wasn't that long of a walk from Hedy's shop, so Ana arrived at the campus after a little bit. She had no idea how long Mel would be or even what classroom she might be in but she thought the chances were good that if she waited out front, near the commons area, Mel might see her waiting there. In any event, she was enjoying being outside.

Students were milling about, some wearing sweatshirts emblazoned with a cartoon hornet, a few wandering around in football jerseys and cheer uniforms. Ana hadn't attended a high school and she found the whole display rather bizarre. She wondered if perhaps the most common use of a high school was to help the students understand that there would be those who were popular, and those who were not, and where exactly each person fit on that sliding scale. It was a depressing thought, really, and Ana shook it from her mind. From the little that Mel had shared about her school experience, she guessed that she was closer to the unpopular side of the scale, which Ana couldn't begin to understand. Mel was smart and funny and talented. If someone like that wasn't popular, there was something wrong with the whole system. Mel was unlike anyone she had ever known.

Ana perched on a bench near the front doors and watched the students coming and going, wishing she had brought a book with her to look less conspicuous. Ana stood out, even when she was doing her best to fly under the radar. Several of the boys wearing football jerseys gave her a look and seemed to be asking themselves who she might be. She noticed a woman with long reddish hair walking away from the school, and she seemed familiar somehow. Maybe she had seen her that night at City Hall. There was something about her that seemed off, but she was too far away for Ana to get a clearer view. A loud buzzer sounded, distracting her, and that seemed to signal a change because the students began to hurry toward the building. Ana was relieved to see the boys head away from her. The woman was gone.

"Waiting for someone?" The voice spoke from behind her and she turned with a start. It was a man, in what looked like a security guard uniform.

"Oh yes, yes I am." The guard walked around the front of the bench so he was looking down on Ana.

"Who are you waiting for?" His voice sounded suspicious even as his square face looked blank.

"Her name is Mel. Mel Stevenson." The guard took out a notepad and jotted something down.

"And what is she to you, exactly?" The guard waited, his pen hovering above the pad.

"Excuse me, but I'm not sure why you are asking me questions. I've done nothing wrong. I'm just sitting here waiting." Ana's voice was polite but she felt irritation rising in her stomach. The guard made a slight clicking noise with his tongue.

"Look, we have the safety of our students to think about and if some stranger, someone who doesn't belong, is sitting outside of the school, I have an obligation to investigate." He clicked his tongue again, looking down at Ana with narrowing eyes.

"Well, as I've said, I am just waiting for Mel. If my being here is a problem, I can go wait across the street, on a public bench." Ana tried to stand up but the guard was standing just a little too close to allow that.

"Why don't we head into the office and we can call the police station. If you are just here waiting for your friend, then there is no reason not to check in with them, right?" The guard reached down and grabbed onto Ana's wrist.

"Hey, what is going on here?" Ana heard the shout of Mel's voice and she turned her head to see her running up to the bench.

"Do you know this person, *Melanie*?" The guard said her full name with a bit more emphasis than was required.

"Yes, Stuart, I do know her. Let go. Jesus, go find something useful to do and leave people alone." Stuart released her hand and backed away from the pair.

"I'm just doing my job, watching out for strangers. If she pulled out some kind of weapon, you'd be thanking me." His eyes were back on the seated figure of Ana.

"How's your application for the police academy going, Stuart? Third time's a charm." Mel took Ana by the arm and led her away from the bench.

"Does Mark know about your 'friend'?" Stuart shouted toward the girls as he stomped back toward the school office.

"Don't pay any attention to Stuart. He's a friend of my older brother, Mark, and he graduated four years ago but he can't seem to get anything going beyond harassing people at school," she paused and then said with a smile, "What are you doing here?"

"I thought I would wait for you to finish your test. I didn't know it would cause such a problem." Ana sounded far away as she spoke. "Is it a crime to just sit on a bench here?"

"No, hey, you didn't do anything wrong. I am glad you came, really. Stuart is just a jerk. He thinks he is important and he couldn't be less so.

Don't let him freak you out. I'm sure he seemed scary, but everything is OK, really." Mel gave another smile and tried to make Ana feel better. The last thing she would want would be for Ana to regret coming to see her. Ana's face softened and she took Mel by the arm, turning left down the sidewalk back toward the house.

"I don't know about this town. So far, I've seen some of the ugliest behavior I've encountered in this country."

"It's crazy, I know. I was born in this town and I don't remember it ever being like this. It used to be an easy-going place. I promise, we aren't all like Stuart."

"Thank goodness for that." The girls laughed and continued strolling back toward Hedy's house. Ana had a few blocks to decide if she was going to be honest with Mel and tell her everything while she still had the courage.

"Ana, I know you aren't going to be here for long but I just wanted you to know how much it has meant to me that I have met you. I've never met anyone like you, anyone it's like I've known my whole life even though we just met. I know that sounds crazy, sorry." Mel had blurted her thoughts out and she instantly regretted it. Ana was nice certainly, but this was taking things too far.

Ana stopped and Mel let go of her arm, turning to face her.

"Please don't apologize. As you say, it has only been a short while but I too feel very comfortable with you. It's because I consider you a friend that I feel I have to be honest with you about who I am, about what I am." She felt her throat tighten up as she tried to speak, afraid equally that her words would stick in her throat or be spoken out loud.

"What do you mean 'what you are'?" The buzzer at the school rang again in the distance.

"You've had a crazy week, meeting me, talking with animals..." the girls both laughed, "... and of course the fires. It's probably too much too soon to tell you this, but I'm not like other girls you have met. I'm quite different actually." Ana wanted to keep walking, to not have to look Mel in the eyes as she spoke but it would be too awkward to pass by Mel who blocked the path.

"Mel, you are smart. No doubt you've sensed that Hedy's house is a bit different. That strange things seem to be centered there, yes?" Mel nodded her head slowly. "OK, well, that isn't a coincidence. Hedy plays host to travelers who need a place to stay, travelers who might have a difficult time staying in hotels or other traditional places." Mel still looked confused and Ana took a deep breath.

"Just spit it out, Ana. What are you trying to tell me?"

"Mel, I'm not strictly human. I'm what is called an undine. I'm a water elemental." She said it. The words were in the air and they couldn't be taken back. The silence that met them was painful.

"What does that mean? Are you some kind of

mermaid? I don't understand." Mel was blinking at Ana, trying to see whatever it was that Ana was trying to tell her but failing. Her voice sounded a bit panicked.

"No, I'm not a mermaid, though that's not far from the truth of it. Elementals like me are tied to the water, we need it to survive. It is hard to explain but trust me when I tell you that I may be different but I'm still like you, that we can still be friends." Ana should have rehearsed her explanation better. She was fumbling around, trying to make herself sound less different, less of something to be feared and it ended up sounded clumsy.

Mel looked at Ana, still confused and not really understanding what Ana meant. She thought she should be afraid, to back away from a person who maybe wasn't really a person. Maybe somewhere in her brain she was afraid, but all she could focus on was that this news didn't really matter. She knew who Ana really was.

"Ana, I don't care. I don't care if you are a water elemental, or from Iran, or really a talking cat. I don't care. You are exactly what you are meant to be and everything about that is fine with me." Mel leaned toward Ana and before either of them knew what was happening, Mel gave her a quick kiss, the first either had ever had. The girls walked hand in hand in silence all the way back to Hedy's shop, both deep in their own thoughts and lost in their moment of happiness.

CHAPTER EIGHTEEN

The door to the fruit cellar had a bad case of English ivy; the invasive vines partially obscuring the dark green door. Bren and Hedy were unobserved by Darro, who was making plans for the dead tree on the other side of the yard.

"We should take care of this while Darro is busy. The less who know, the better." Bren had made the suggestion as they entered the house post-rager with Mr. Jeffries and Hedy had agreed. There was no interior access to the cellar; they would have to move the box in sight of the street.

"Let me get a plastic bag to put the box inside." Hedy had earlier brought the box downstairs and stashed it under the dining room table, hiding it under the flounce of the lace tablecloth. She had already placed the box inside a pillow case, and now she found a large black garbage bag and she tucked it inside, before tying it shut. *That should keep out any curious bugs or vermin, at least,* she hoped. She had wondered if keeping the box in the cellar was the right decision but if Lyssa came back to search the house, it was safer in there.

Bren and Hedy came back out and down to the side of the house, with Bren carrying the box under his arm. The good news was that this side of the house was not in view of Mr. Jeffries' home; they could both imagine that he was still frothing at the mouth, watching Darro work in the yard and encroach on his property.

The fruit cellar had an old rusted chain and lock, which Bren was able to remove after a moment of warming up the iron with his palm, which was good because Hedy didn't have the key. It fell loosely into the ivy and Hedy pulled open the door, releasing the stale scent of damp earth, spider egg sacs and musty corners. No one had been in this cellar in years.

With her flashlight turned on, she stepped gingerly into the cellar, making sure she stomped her foot as she went down each stair. Whatever might be living down here was given full warning of their entrance. The gray light from the open door spilled in but much of the cellar was still in darkness. After a moment, Bren found a chain and gave it a tug, filling the space with dull yellow light.

"Well, that's handy." Hedy almost preferred the darkness. The light made very clear the layers of cobwebs and filthy old canning jars that lined the shelves.

"Here, there's a cubby hole under this shelf, back in the corner. The box should fit perfectly." Bren took the crate from under his arm and nestled it into the hole; it just barely fit. He took a remnant of cardboard and placed it in front of the box.

"Ok, that should do it. This would be the last place anyone would look." Bren and Hedy gladly stepped back up the steps and into the light, quickly shutting the green door behind them. From her apron pocket, Hedy pulled out a new padlock and placed it on the old iron latch. She hoped no one would notice it.

"I doubt the lock would keep anyone out if they were determined but it might keep casual looky-loos away." Hedy dusted her hands against her apron and headed back toward the front of the house. Neither of them happened to notice the reddish tail peeking out of the English ivy.

* * *

The afternoon was a busy one. Mel and Ana had returned, looking for all the world like it was the best day of their lives. They sat at Mel's table, sipping tea and talking with their heads together. Hedy didn't mean to watch them so closely but she hardly left the counter, with the influx of customers. Even if Halloween was three weeks away, word had gotten out about the quirky bake shop on Griffin avenue with the foxtail donuts and the yeti paw treats. Apparently, the local newspaper, the Enumclaw Courier-Herald, found the shop interesting because they sent a reporter to interview Hedy for a feature they were planning to run in the Halloween edition of the paper.

"Do you mind if I ask you a few questions, in between customers?" The man they sent to interview her was young, hardly older than Mel it seemed to Hedy.

"That's fine, as long as you don't mind some interruptions. I have to get more cookies in the oven." Hedy had a tray of kraken cookies ready to bake, with more dough on the marble slab.

"Not at all, it will give me a chance to take a few pictures while I am here. So, your name is Hedy Leckermaul, correct? And you moved to Enumclaw just last year to open this shop, The Gingerbread Hag. Interesting name for a bakery." He looked at her expectantly but Hedy was waiting for a question.

"Why do you make such strange treats? What's the thinking behind rat shaped cookies?"

"Well, to some they might be strange, but to others they are fascinating. Anyone can make a plain old round sugar cookie. What's the fun in that?" The kraken cookies were in the oven and the timer set, just as another pair of customers approached the counter. The reporter waited patiently as Hedy boxed up the fresh banana bread and six of the iced withered leaf cookies.

"Business is brisk today but you haven't done much in the way of advertising. You barely have a small sign out front and I haven't seen or heard any kind of ad for the shop. How are folks hearing about you?"

"I'm assuming by word of mouth. Opening the shop has been a labor of love. The Leckermauls have a history as bakers, all the way back to the Black Forest in Germany. If I didn't bake, I wouldn't know what to do with myself."

"Why Enumclaw to open up your shop? Surely you could have done better in an urban place like Seattle or Tacoma."

"Why not Enumclaw? Who says that only big cities can have interesting things? In all seriousness, I have lived in many cities for many years and I was ready for a slower, calmer pace of life. Enumclaw seemed like a perfect place to slow down and concentrate of my baking."

"Hard to say that right now with all the missing women and the fires, huh? Though thank goodness that has come to end." The reporter had his camera out to snap a picture of a red velvet cake with a candy hatchet through the top, when Hedy stopped him.

"What do you mean, it has come to end?" Mel and Ana had stopped their chatting and were paying close attention as well.

"Oh, I suppose it hasn't made the news yet but I heard just as I was coming here on the police band that they have made an arrest for the arsons. Some homeless man was found with a bag belonging to one of the missing women."

"Really? I wonder why he would set the fires and what happened to the women?" Hedy asked.

"I'm sure we'll learn more when the police issue

their statement. I'm still on the lifestyle beat so I won't be covering it." He sounded disappointed. Just then Bren came into the shop, followed by a ruddy faced Darro, finished with his rose wrangling for the day. He brought the smell of damp garden trailing behind him.

"The police think they have caught the arsonist, a homeless man." Hedy said and she saw the surprise on Bren's face; it matched her own.

"If it is alright with you, can we finish the interview? I need to get over to the meat market to interview them about making sausage for Octoberfest." The reporter really sounded like he hated his job.

"Certainly. What else would you like to know?"

Hedy and the reporter chatted while Bren and Darro joined the girls at the table. Darro was waiting for his pay but he figured he might as well be sociable while he did so. Bren and Ana hadn't spoken since the confrontation last night but he spoke as if he didn't seem inclined to hold a grudge.

"Here's a quick blurb about it on the Internet. 'A homeless man, name unknown at this time, has been arrested in the recent arson and missing persons cases in Enumclaw, WA this week. The man's connection to the two missing women is unknown. He was reportedly found with a backpack belonging to one of the women and was identified as at the scene just prior to the first fire. Police have no comment at this time but will be releasing a statement.' That's all there is." Mel read from the screen on her phone.

"How would a homeless man abduct two women? It doesn't make any sense." Bren shook his head, clearly not finding the story plausible.

Darro chimed in. "We don't know all the facts, do we. He might have had help, he might have some vehicle that he used. I'm sure the police will have more information." While not necessarily a fan of the police in general, especially before pot was legal, he saw no reason to doubt the news of the arrest.

"I'm glad to hear it. Maybe now that the danger is passed, people will settle down and stop acting like idiots." Mel looked meaningfully at Ana and Bren wondered what that was all about.

The reporter had wrapped up his questions and taken a few pictures of the shop, with Hedy doing her best to pose in her polka dot apron, holding a rolling pin. If she had known about the interview, she would have taken the time to have fixed up her hair; it would just have to do.

"Thank you for your time. You'll be in the Halloween issue of the paper. No surprise there, huh?" The reporter headed out the door, giving the shop one last look and a shrug as he headed out the front door.

"I suppose I should be offended by that comment. As if I'm only suitable for Halloween." The timer dinged for the kraken cookies and Hedy grabbed her oven mitt.

CHAPTER NINETEEN

"I'd say it has been a good day then, all considered. Darro managed not to trade blows with Jeffries next door. The police think they have the arsonist in custody, and I have just about sold out of everything in the showcase today." Hedy wiped her hands on her apron before switching the Open sign to Closed. She came back to the shop where everyone but Darro, who had left for his nightly hobby, was still at the table.

"Mel, will you be joining us for dinner? Not that we wouldn't love to have you but I don't want your family to think we are taking advantage." Hedy said while Ana looked apprehensively at Mel to hear her reply.

"Actually, I do need to be heading out. My mom sent me a text that she brought home take and bake pizza, so it's a home cooked dinner with the family." She smiled as she said it; Mel's mother was notoriously a bad cook. "Ana, would you like to come over for dinner?" Mel was hoping she would but also fearful about it; she rarely had anyone over to the house, especially someone she liked as well as Ana.

"Oh, well, I don't know...I mean, would your mother mind?" Ana was stalling a bit as she thought about it. She wanted to go but she didn't want another experience like she had with Stuart, the school security guard.

"No, she wouldn't mind at all. I'll send her a text that I'm bringing a friend, and the good news is even my goofy brother won't be there. He's in Seattle trying to get his dumb band off the ground."

"Well, sure then. I would be delighted to join you." Ana smiled and the girls started gathering their things to go. Hedy looked around the showcase and saw that she had a few items left she could pack up.

"Here, take these treats to your mother, with my compliments. I hope that she can come by the shop and visit us sometime." Hedy filled a box with a few of the kraken cookies, a slice of banana bread, and a small pumpkin tart. "Do you girls need a ride?"

"No, it's not rainy, let's walk." Mel took the box from Hedy with a thank you and together they headed off into the twilight.

"That's nice to see, isn't it?" Hedy came back to the table where Bren was deep in thought.

"Oh, yes, I mean, sure." He clearly had hardly noticed their departure.

"What's on your mind this evening, Bren?"

"Something doesn't add up, Hedy. This arrest

makes no sense to me. Why would this man burn down both places and seemingly abduct two women, without a trace? Where did he take them? *How* did he take them?"

"I have no idea, Bren. It's surprising for sure but I'm sure the police have evidence we don't know about. If it turns out that this man didn't do it, then they'll let him go. For now, I'm just glad that this seems to be behind the town." Hedy hadn't felt this relieved in days and she didn't want to let that go, even if the story did seem a bit strange to believe.

"For the sake of the town, I hope they do have the right man but it just doesn't feel right to me. The rage in that fire, remember I can feel that rage even in the embers and ash left behind, that rage had to come from someone who really wanted to see those buildings burn."

Before Hedy could answer him, Zelda came into the shop in a hurry. "Hedy, you might want to come outside."

Zelda led them down the front porch and around to the side of the house. The green fruit cellar door was swung open, one of the hinges loose. In the darkness, she could just make out the lock in the grass.

"Oh no! When did this happen?" Hedy watched as Bren carefully stepped into the dark cellar, fishing around for the light chain. After a few moments, the room had bright light spilling out. She came to the edge of the cellar in time to see Bren shaking his head.

"It's gone. Nothing else has been moved." Bren pulled the light chain and came back out of the cellar.

"Well, damn it. That didn't take long. How the hell did the thief know where we hid it?" She watched Bren as he carefully placed the half-hanging door back over the cellar.

"Maybe he knows something." Zelda gestured toward the patch of ivy where the reddish heap of Ren was laying still.

Hedy came over to the fox and he didn't move. He was barely alive.

"Hedy, careful. He might bite you." Bren watched as she took off her apron and wrapped it carefully around the fox before picking him up. He stirred slightly but otherwise was limp in her hands.

"Let's get him inside." Hedy led the way back into the house, carrying the still fox carefully in her arms.

She brought him into the entry and turned left, into a small room off the entry that had a large octagon table. Carefully, she placed the fox on the table and then turned on the overhead light. The fox was barely breathing but he was alive.

"What happened to the creature?" Bren was beside her, seeing no wounds or marks of damage on its body.

"I don't know. Watch him for a minute while I gather up a few things." She retreated toward the back of the house and came back with a flannel blanket, a chair pad, and a small bottle with an eyedropper. "Lift him up for a minute so I can put the pad underneath him." Bren gingerly lifted the fox, clearly not convinced it was a good idea to have a wounded wild animal in his arms, no matter how still it looked. He placed the fox back down and watched as Hedy loosely covered the fox with the flannel blanket.

"I want to try to get some water down him. Do you think you could hold open his mouth while I drop some inside?"

"No, I don't think that is a good idea, Hedy. Better to let him rest and if he is better in a few hours, we can put out a bowl for him to drink from. Prying open the mouth of a wounded fox is not the best idea, wouldn't you agree?"

Hedy nodded. For now, there wasn't anything they could do other than hope that the fox recovered. She dimmed the overhead light and closed the pocket doors that led into the little room, leaving the fox to rest in the flannel blanket and the two humans to wonder whether he would recover or die on Hedy's table.

CHAPTER TWENTY

A couple of hours passed and Ana had not returned from dinner with Mel. Hedy kept checking on the fox but so far, he didn't appear to be stirring. There wasn't an emergency vet in town, and she doubted whether the vet would treat a wild fox anyway.

With the showcase in the shop so empty, she had some midnight baking ahead of her to be ready for the morning. Bren asked if he could help so the two of them donned aprons and set to work.

"We'll need some cookies, a quick bread like banana or pumpkin, two batches of cupcakes or muffins, and some hand pies." Hedy was eyeing the double ovens in the shop and calculating temperature to maximize the baking time.

"That sounds like a lot." Bren had never so much as iced a cookie but he was willing to be helpful.

"It is a lot, normally I don't have to do quite so much at one time - I can bake a few things throughout the day and keep the shelf restocked, with a larger batch now and then. But we can get as far as we want tonight and then I'll do some more in the morning."

"So, where do we start?" Bren asked.

"I have quite a bit of pie dough already chilled in the fridge, so we can start there, rolling out rounds for hand pies. Pumpkin seems like a good filling for the season." Hedy put Bren on the task of making the filling. Rather than roasting a fresh pumpkin, she actually preferred the taste and texture of canned pumpkin for her pies. Bren had can after can to open, plopping the orange puree into a large ceramic bowl.

"OK, you have a vat of pumpkin here, what do I do with it?"

"Time to flavor it up with spices. Over on the shelf there, grab the cinnamon, clove, nutmeg, and ginger. You'll need the salt cellar and the sugar jar as well." Hedy walked him through adding all the spices and sweetening it up with sugar. "We'll beat up some eggs and add that to your pumpkin, and then we are ready to add some filling to the dough I have rolled out."

The front door bell tinkled and both Hedy and Bren looked up, expecting to see Ana. It was a police officer instead.

"Good evening, how can I help you?" Hedy rubbed her hands off on the apron and came around to the front of the shop.

"Officer Williams, ma'am. I am here because your neighbor, Mr. Jeffries, lodged a complaint today about an altercation he claims he had with you. I'm here to take your statement."

"Please come in, Officer. I am sorry you had to come over something like this. It was nothing on our part, anyway. Mr. Jeffries became livid over the removal of some rose bushes on my property."

"Yes, he told me about the bushes and to be honest, I'm not that interested about whether or not the bushes belong to you or him; he can take that up in small claims court if he wants. I'm here to discuss the threats he says were made."

"Threats? What threats?" Bren had removed his apron and come around to join the pair.

"Who are you, sir? Do you live here?" The officer had his notebook out and ready.

"My name is Bren Aldebrand, I'm a friend of Ms. Leckermaul and I am just staying here for a few days. I was present at the confrontation with Mr. Jeffries this morning."

"He claims that two men and Ms. Leckermaul threatened him with physical harm. He said one of them, who had a slight German accent, said 'I'm going to knock your head into the pavement, old man.' Did you say that, Mr. Aldebrand?"

"Absolutely not. No one said anything like that to Mr. Jeffries. No threats were made. Ms. Leckermaul informed him that he wasn't welcome on her property but that was it." Bren looked astonished by the claim, as did Hedy. The officer jotted down Bren's statement.

"Ms. Leckermaul, who is the man that was with you that had a Scottish accent? Is he here?"

"That would be Darro, the gardener that I hired, at Mr. Jeffries' insistence, I might add. Darro was with us but he said nothing threatening either. I have his phone number if you wish to contact him."

"Yes, thank you ma'am. I'll need his statement as well. I will tell you that Mr. Jeffries is quite adamant that he felt threatened and that he is going to request a restraining order against you. I can't say whether such an order will be granted but you will likely have to appear in court." The officer closed his notebook, his face a blank slate.

"It's really ridiculous, Officer. No one has ever threatened Mr. Jeffries and if truth be told, he has been the one that has imposed himself on me, time after time, complaining about trivial things. I'll appear in court if that is required but if he continues harassing me, I'll be forced to get a lawyer involved."

Officer Williams headed for the front door and passed Ana on the porch as she was coming in. She looked surprised and was even more so when she heard why the officer had stopped by.

"That man is crazy. Honestly, what is he trying to do?" Ana took off her jacket and hung it on the rack in the entry.

"I don't know, but he is the least of our worries tonight. Someone took the Greek crate." Hedy slid open the pocket door to reveal Ren, the fox, still curled up in the flannel blanket.

"What happened to him? Who took the box?"

Ana peered inside the blanket and watched Ren's shallow breathing.

"We're hoping he can tell us that, when he wakes up. Whoever took it knew exactly where we had it hidden."

"Could be your crazy neighbor. He probably took it and hurt the fox. I wouldn't put either past him." Ana gave the fox a soft touch and she felt him stir slightly. She didn't seem the least bit concerned that she was petting a wounded, wild animal.

"Hedy, he moved. I think he is waking up." Ana said. The three gathered around the table and watched the fox for several minutes, as Ana gently stroked his fur. After several minutes, the fox began to blink slowly.

"Ren. Ren, you are alright. You are here in the house, you were injured." Hedy tried to speak calmly so the fox wouldn't panic and possibly bite them in fear.

Ren's eyes widened and he looked around at the human faces peering down at him. He rustled slightly and gingerly sat up.

"What am I doing in here?" He shuffled off the flannel blanket and blinked at the overhead light.

"We found you outside, in the ivy, unconscious. We brought you inside to warm up and hopefully wake up." Hedy watched the fox carefully shake his head, stretching out his neck from side to side.

"Oh yes, I remember now. The lady." He said.

"The lady? Did someone hurt you?" Hedy asked.

"Do you have some water?" He lightly licked his parched lips. His voice sounded raspy.

"Yes, of course, here you go." Hedy had a saucer of water on the edge of the bookshelf and she passed it over to the large table where Ren sat.

"Thank you." He lapped the water slowly before continuing. "Yes, I was out in the shrubs near the side of the house, where I had a nice juicy mole caught, when I heard a lady speak. She said 'I see you little fox, I see you there. Come out, come out and tell me what I need to know.' I honestly thought it was you, Miss." Ren paused and took another sip of water.

"What did she look like?" Ana took over the questioning.

"Dark eyes, pitch black and no light at all. Long reddish hair, I think, but the eyes were all I could see. I heard crows cawing as she spoke." Ren gave a slight shudder as he remembered those black eyes.

"What did she do then?" Hedy knew why he seemed shaken; she had seen those eyes herself.

"I came out from the shrubs, I still had the mole by the scruff of his neck in my teeth, and then I felt her hand around my neck. I couldn't move. I tried to move, to run, but it was like I was trapped in those eyes of hers. She held me by the neck and I felt limp. She asked me where the woman with the white hair had hidden the box."

"How did you know?" Bren found himself questioning a fox and he wasn't sure he had ever been in a more surreal conversation.

"I saw you both place the box behind that door. You weren't exactly quiet about it. With my ears, I could have heard you a block away. I told the woman what she wanted to know and then I felt her tighten her hold on me. Then I woke up in here." He took another sip of water and gingerly moved his neck one more time.

"I'm sorry that happened to you, Ren. She used you to get what she wanted from me. We thought hiding it in the cellar would be the last place she would look but we obviously didn't give her enough credit." Hedy took the empty saucer from the table and headed back toward the open pocket doors.

"You are welcome to stay inside tonight, you should rest up." She looked back at the fox but she could tell he was anxious to leave the house; he was done with humans for the night.

"Thank you, but no, I would rather go to my den. My family is no doubt worried about me. I hope never to lay eyes on that woman again. I'm sorry if telling your secret has caused you any problem." Ren hopped down from the table and followed Hedy into the hallway.

"That's just it, we don't know why she wanted that box, and now I'm afraid to find out." Hedy opened the front door and Ren passed through to the front porch and into the night, away from the house.

CHAPTER TWENTY-ONE

Hedy was up earlier than usual, busy in the kitchen and busy in her thoughts. She hadn't been able to sleep. Lyssa's assault against the fox and taking the crate from the cellar made it clear that more danger was to come. She had decided to accept no more travelers for the time being; she had already called the Concierge to let them know that, for now, the Enumclaw waystation was closed. Now she had to decide whether to ask Ana and Bren to leave.

Her hands were kneading the dough and her mind was playing out the conversation. They would object, they would be hurt, they would argue against why sending them away made sense. And in truth, all their arguments would make sense. They knew the danger and if they chose to stay, that was their informed choice. But Hedy felt certain it was the wrong choice. Her gut told her that Lyssa wasn't done with them and every time she had dismissed her gut, she had been sorry - both now and in the past.

"No peace I feel in this house." Adelaide's voice drifted into the kitchen, which was unusual; she usually kept to the second floor or the entry at most.

"You are right, Adelaide. No peace indeed." She had hoped making bread would calm her down, the rhythm of the kneading, the feel of the smooth dough under her floured hands, but she still felt on edge.

"Danger is here, I feel it. Danger to she, danger from he." Adelaide's voice drifted away, leaving Hedy even more frustrated than before.

"Why must you speak in riddles, Adelaide? That is no help!" The ghost didn't answer and Hedy slammed the dough into the countertop and walked away.

Who was the 'she'? Was it Hedy, was it Mel or Ana? Maybe it was someone who hadn't even arrived yet. And the 'he'? The police had a man in custody for the fires. Did she mean Bren or Jeffries? And why no mention of Lyssa? Nothing Adelaide had said made any sense.

"Hedy? Everything alright?" Ana came into the kitchen and surveyed the scene.

"No, Ana. Everything isn't alright, unfortunately. There is too much danger around this house right now. I think it might be best if you and Bren went on to your next waystations, away from here."

Ana was shaking her head before Hedy even finished speaking. "No, I don't want to leave. Whatever this Lyssa creature wants, I'm not leaving you to the danger alone. You are mortal, Hedy. At least I think you are..." Ana gave a cheeky smile, which made Hedy smile in return. "Your best defense against whatever Lyssa has planned is to have some extra help from me and Bren. I'm staying even if you toss me out." She took both of Hedy's flour-covered hands in hers and gave them a squeeze.

"Ana, I appreciate that, I really do, but if something happened to you or Bren, or anyone connected with this house, I wouldn't forgive myself. I'm hoping that now that she has the box, she'll move on and leave us alone but what if she doesn't? What if there is more she has planned? It is too much to ask."

"No, it isn't." Bren had entered the room and he chimed in before Ana could speak. "I assume you are trying to persuade Ana to leave. I can't speak for her but I am not leaving, not while this woman is still around here." He joined them at the kitchen table, looking like he too hadn't slept much.

"You both are very kind, really. But I want you to think about this today and really be sure. I would feel relieved if you decide to leave, then I would know you were safe."

"Well, call me selfish then, but I am not leaving and you will just have to know that someone has your back." Ana gave Hedy a hug and then let go awkwardly; she wasn't adept at physical affection.

"Agreed. I'm in this until the end." Bren said simply.

"I can see that talking to you two is getting me nowhere, so I'll get back to my bread." But she said it with a soft voice, her eyes close to tears. She had relied on herself alone for so long, after everything that had happened to her over the years, it felt unnatural to have friends who would stand by her side even in danger.

"Hedy, do you have a traveler mug?" Ana chuckled at the unintended pun. "Mel has another test this morning, so I am going to walk to the school and wait for her to finish. I thought I would take some coffee with me."

"Hmmm, yes, I think I might have one. I think the bank gave it to me when I opened an account last year." Hedy rummaged around in the cupboards until she found an insulated tumbler. Hedy hated drinking out of plastic, so it had never been used. She gave it a rinse from the tap and filled it up with hot coffee.

"Maybe I should walk with you. I could pick up a newspaper to see if there are any updates on the man in custody." Bren still had the arsonist on his mind.

"Oh, I can bring you back a paper. You should stay here and keep an eye on things. I'll be back with Mel in a little while; she only has the one test to take. I will be fine." Ana hadn't told them about the encounter with Stuart.

Bren nodded and poured himself a cup of coffee. He felt better with the idea of being close by the house. He didn't want to worry Hedy but he didn't think Lyssa was done with them yet.

"Alright then, see you later then." Ana raised her tumbler in farewell and headed toward the front door.

* * *

The morning bustled by, faster than Hedy could believe. She was busy with baking, with customers, and with Darro who seemed to have a million questions about what kinds of bulbs she wanted planted for the spring. She hadn't had time to notice that Mel and Ana hadn't yet returned.

Bren had spent his morning exploring Hedy's library, looking particularly for any books on Greek mythology. Now and then, a cold breeze would ruffle the pages of his book but there were no other signs of Adelaide's presence in the room. It wasn't until his stomach started to grumble that he realized it was late morning.

Coming down the stairs, he saw the front door open and Mel come in. "Hello, Mel. How was the test?" She waited for him to reach her and they went into the shop together.

"You mean tests. I had two today. I told Ana there was no sense in waiting for me, I would just meet her here when they were over. Where is she?" Hedy had joined them from behind the counter.

"She isn't back. We thought she was with you. When did you see her?"

Mel looked at her watch. "It's one-thirty now, I saw her at the break between the tests, about two hours ago. She was heading back then." Mel and Hedy both looked worried; there was no way it would take two hours to walk back from the school.

Bren spoke up. "Let's not panic, alright? She might have decided to window shop or stop by the library or get a bite to eat. I'll take the car and look around town while you both wait here for her." Hedy walked over to the small drawer by the cash register and pulled out the keys for Bren.

"I should go with you." Mel started toward the door but Hedy reached out and held onto her arm.

"Wait here with me, OK, Mel? Bren can search and you can be here when she walks through that front door. I'm sure she'll be here any time." Hedy lied with conviction. Mel didn't believe Hedy but they both nodded and watched Bren take off through the front door.

"Let's have some tea and you can tell me how dinner went last night with your mother."

* * *

Bren came back after a long hour with no news of Ana. He had hoped to find her, but it seemed a bit of long shot. Ana didn't strike him as the kind of girl who would window shop in a small town. He had only really held out hope that she was at the library, perhaps doing some research as he had been, but there was no sign of her and when asked about a small young woman with long dark hair, the librarian hadn't seen her.

"No luck? We haven't heard anything." Hedy met him at the door. Ana didn't have a cell phone, as many of those like her did not. Modern technology held less appeal to elementals and those of a supernatural nature. Bren was beginning to think that was a mistake on their part.

"We better call the police." Bren came into the shop, watching the fretful Mel as she quickly scanned her phone for any shred of news she might find.

"And tell them that an undine has gone missing?" Mel didn't look up from her phone as she spoke. Clearly, she knew the truth about Ana.

"The fact that she is an undine doesn't have to be discussed, only that she is missing. We can use their help to find her." Bren sat down at the table with Mel who still didn't look up.

"Maybe she left town. Maybe she decided this was all too much and she would rather just move on." Mel had tears at the corners of her eyes, ready to flow at any moment.

"I checked her room. Her things are still here. She wouldn't leave her things. And she wouldn't leave without saying goodbye. You know that." Hedy came over to the table to try to keep Mel calm.

"Let's retrace her steps. Let's walk to the school on the route she would use and see if we can find anything that will help." Bren took the phone from Mel's hands and she finally looked up.

"OK, let's try that." She replied in a small voice and left her phone on the table as she gathered up her coat. The three of them headed out to the sidewalk.

"Everything a'ight?" Darro came up from the back of the house where he had been working for the last few hours.

"No, our friend Ana is missing. She walked to the high school and she hasn't come back yet." Bren kept his voice measured and calm as he spoke, hoping it would help Mel's nerves.

"Oh, that's terrible. Shall I come w' ye?" He dropped the spade he was holding and dusted his hands off on his coveralls.

"No, but it would be helpful if you stayed here in case she comes back. It shouldn't take us that long to walk the route. If we don't find anything, we'll be back and call the police."

"Well, keep your head, young miss. It will turn out right, I have a feeling in my gut, and you can trust a gut this size." Darro slapped his belly but Mel couldn't muster a smile.

The trio took off in the afternoon light, heading along Griffin Avenue toward the high school, looking for any sign of Anahita on the way.

CHAPTER TWENTY-TWO

Mel had led them along the route they had taken before, walking to Garfield Street, then down to Roosevelt, and finally Semanski Street. It wasn't a long walk, through the residential neighborhood but the group moved slowly, looking for any sign of Ana on the way. A few people were out in their yards and Hedy took the opportunity to ask them if they had seen Ana. Mel kicked herself that she hadn't brought her phone because she could have shown them a picture, the selfie they had taken together just last night at dinner.

"No, I haven't seen anyone who looks like that," the older woman sweeping her walkway said when asked. "I'd remember someone who looks like that, certainly. Girls today all have those short haircuts that look like boys, like yours," gesturing to Mel. Hedy thanked her and they continued on toward the school.

Class was out for the day and students were milling around, waiting for buses or cars to pick them up. Mel showed them the bench where she had met Ana just that morning, and she sat down in the spot where Ana had been waiting for her.

Bren looked around and saw there really wasn't anything around them that would have caught Ana's eye, no shops or places of interest that she would have wandered over to instead of heading back to the shop. They did a small sweep around the bench, fanning out in a circle to make sure nothing was there, but it didn't take long to see that Ana had left no trace there at the school. Mel even hunted down Stuart to ask if he knew anything, but as she expected, he was no help.

"Let's head back. She would have walked the same route I expect." Mel nodded yes to the question; it was the only route that Ana knew.

"If she isn't back at the shop, let's call the police." Bren led the way, with Mel to his left and Hedy looking toward the right. It was still daylight but the light was getting a bit dimmer in the later afternoon. Soon it would be night.

There wasn't a trace of Ana on Semanski, or Roosevelt or Garfield, and they turned back onto Griffin Avenue, heading back to the shop. They had to pass Jeffries' house and Hedy noticed that it was dark, not so much as a porch light on in the darkening afternoon light. While she was noticing this fact, she saw it, there by the front gate.

Hedy stopped, kneeling down and pushing back the leaf that partially obscured the necklace. Ana's small vial of water, the one she wore around her neck at all times, was on the sidewalk next to

Jeffries' gate. They had missed it earlier.

"What have you found?" Mel squatted down and then make a small gasp. She immediately recognized the necklace.

"Ana's necklace." Hedy picked it up and held it out in her palm for Bren. The silver chain was snapped in half.

"She was here, she must have made it all the way back and something happened here." Bren picked up the vial and turned it over in his hand.

Before Hedy or Bren knew what was happening, Mel had run passed Jeffries' gate and was pounding on his front door.

"Open up. Hey, open up!" She yelled at the door, loud enough that Darro heard her and came running around from the side of the house.

The house was dark and Mel's pounding went unanswered.

"I dinna think he is at home. Quite a bit before you came out for your walk, I saw his station wagon heading down the street at a brisk pace. He drove like the devil himself was chasing him, the daft codger."

Mel let Hedy lead her off the porch and they walked back over to the house to consider what to do next.

Bren was the first to speak. "OK, I think we can say that Jeffries might know something about Ana since the necklace was found right by his gate. I think I should go inside the house and look around. Maybe there will be something that will lead us to Ana."

"You are gonna break in, then?" Darro seemed surprise that someone as prim and proper as Bren would consider breaking and entering.

"I don't think we have a choice. We could call the police, tell them about the necklace but that doesn't give them enough evidence to go inside. They will say she could have lost it on her way to the school. There is nothing connecting her to Jeffries."

"Do it. We'll keep watch for him coming back. Take my phone and we'll call you from Hedy's house phone if he returns." Mel said before she ran inside and returned with her phone from the table.

Bren took the phone, sliding it into his pocket. He walked back toward Jeffries' yard. He was hoping there was a back door to the small bungalow, and sure enough, as he made his way around the meticulous side garden, he saw a back porch and wooden door leading into the back of the house.

Bren climbed the stairs and peered into the dark window next to the door, making sure there was no one inside. He took a deep breath and placed his hand on the metal knob, gripping it tightly. Focusing all his energy on his hand, he felt the knob heat up and saw the faint glow of the metal. It was now malleable enough to bend and he gave the knob a sharp twist, making the knob torque out of shape and the lock snap in half. The door pulled open.

Bren entered what appeared to be a kitchen and found a light switch on the wall. The light came on and he could see that the house hadn't been updated since it was built in the 1920s. Rather than charming, it had a neglected and worn look about it that was depressing. He passed through the small opening into a dining room and found another light switch. The dining room table was strewn with papers and clippings from the local paper. It looked like it hadn't been cleaned in years; even the air smelled like layers of dust and cobwebs. But there was another scent that Bren recognized; the scent of coming fire.

Bren glanced over the papers and saw clippings about the legalization of marijuana, Washington's marriage equality act, news from a gay pride parade, the opening of the Sandy Bottoms bikini barista stand, and right on top, articles about the recent fires. Each article was marked up with a red pen, words circled or crossed out, lines drawn and scrawled phrases of "hell is coming" and "trash" in large letters.

Bren left the disturbing piles of paper and headed into the front room. From the windows on the left he could see Hedy's yard. No doubt Jeffries had perched in here and watched with anger at the comings and goings at the house. But why had he abducted Ana?

"My, my, if it isn't the salamander. How nice to meet you." A female voice spoke from behind him and he whirled around to face her. She stood near the dining room table with all the clippings. Her dark eyes were all that Bren could really focus on, though he was aware of her reddish hair moving about her despite the still, fetid air.

"We haven't been properly introduced. My name is Lyssa. What brings a salamander to this sleepy little town, eh?" Her hand lightly swirled around some of the pages on the table.

Bren could hardly force himself to reply. Those eyes were drawing him in.

"Just passing through. But now I need to find my friend."

Lyssa laughed softly, her voice would have been beautiful in any other context. "Oh, you mean the undine? Yes, what a stroke of luck for an undine to cross my path. She's a lovely girl, isn't? I'll be making her acquaintance soon." She ran her finger along the edge of her long black coat.

"Where is she? Tell me where she is." Bren took a step toward Lyssa and she smiled.

"Oh, there's no fun in telling you where she is. I'm not through with her yet. She'll be back when I have no more need of her. But right now, I need to attend to my unwitting helper. He should be back any moment."

Bren took another step toward Lyssa, though he had no idea what he would do if he reached her.

"Your helper? Jeffries? He took Ana."

"Yes, he took the undine, at my direction. Though he didn't realize it was for me. Everything he has done has been at my direction, a little voice just giving him a nudge. Not that he needs much help in that direction." She scattered the pages again. "His hate is palpable and that makes him pliable, easy to use. Having such a willing helper makes my task that much easier." Lyssa took a step toward Bren and now they were practically face to face.

"I don't want to hurt you but I will if you don't tell me where Ana is." Bren's temperature began to rise, though he still had it under his control, for now.

Lyssa laughed merrily. "Oh, my dear salamander. You are too much. As if you, an elemental, could hurt me, the daughter of Nyx, the dark goddess of the night. Really, how very amusing, almost amusing as these mortals. They are so susceptible to whispers of rage and madness. I find it almost too easy to stir their passions, their basest fears." Lyssa's eyes flashed darkly and Bren found that her hands were now around his throat. He couldn't move.

"My dear salamander, I have no need for you. Once my little helper returns, I will deal with him and make the acquaintance of the lovely little undine. Farewell, salamander." Bren felt her hands tight on his throat and everything in front of his eyes began to turn reddish black. He felt himself sinking to the ground, sinking into those dark eyes.

CHAPTER TWENTY-THREE

There was smoke, all around him. Smoke and heat and the smell of kerosene. This fire was newly born, not fully engulfing the house but it would in a few minutes. Bren tried to clear the darkness from his brain and wake himself up. Next to him was the limp body of Jeffries.

Bren coughed and tried to clear his head but the smoke swirled in his eyes, in his lungs. He reached out a hand and gave the still body a shake. He heard a weak groan coming from the man; he was still alive.

"We have to get out of here." He croaked out the words as the fire began to roar around them. "Jeffries, wake up." He shook the body again and again he heard the slight moan.

Bren pocket was vibrating and it took him a minute to realize that Mel's phone was ringing. He didn't have time to answer it, they only had seconds to get out of the house. He lumbered to his feet, still dazed and moving like he was bound to the warped floorboards.

Jeffries was barely breathing and it was all that Bren could do to bend over and pull the lifeless man to a sitting position so he could sling him over his shoulder. He hoped he had enough strength to carry them both out of the fire. Jeffries moaned as Bren hoisted him up and he headed toward the front door. The fire was all around them but heaviest toward the back of the house. The papers that had littered the dining room table were wisps of ash. With the heat of this fire, there would be nothing left. The smell of Lyssa's delight permeated the smoke.

Bren grabbed a throw blanket off the sofa as he passed it, trying to cover Jeffries and shield him from the heat. The man screamed in pain, though his voice was muffled by the flannel blanket over his head.

"Hold on, Jeffries. Just a few more feet." Bren staggered toward the door and gave it a kick with all his might. The flames were all around them and though he didn't feel the pain, his clothes were starting to burn on his body. Jeffries was now writhing on his shoulder.

The door was holding and Bren gave it one last kick before it finally opened and he was able to see the front porch and the darkness in front of him. He felt the fire roar behind him as the oxygen from outside poured into the house. He managed the few more steps until he could stumble down the front porch and creep toward the front walkway. He could just make out the shapes of people gathered on the sidewalk, before his knees buckled and Jeffries tumbled to the walkway.

He felt Darro's hands under his armpits, dragging him away from the fire and he was on the cool damp grass near the street. Hedy was hovering above him and he felt Jeffries' hot body pulled next to him.

"Bren, are you alright? Say something!" Hedy's voice was sharp with worry.

"Save Jeffries. He knows...Ana...danger." Bren croaked out the words, finding that the smoke he had swallowed had closed up his throat. Salamanders in their human form could suffocated in fire, and he very nearly had.

Mel was wiping down Jeffries with wet towels and with each stroke the man howled, his skin blood red from the burns. "Lass, don't touch him. He's badly burned. Pour some water down his gullet if you can." Darro's voice carried over the sound of the crackling flames. Bren could hear the distant sound of a fire truck.

"Where is she, Jeffries? Where is Ana?" Hedy was standing over the burned man, revolted by the peeling skin and the shrieks of pain coming from him.

"Too late. The cabin. Too late." He croaked the words before he lost consciousness.

"The cabin? Where, what cabin?" Hedy yelled into his ear but he said no more. Mel grabbed her arm and pulled her away.

"Come on, I can find it." Mel reached into Bren's

pocket for her phone; luckily, it hadn't melted. Both women raced back toward the house while Bren stayed where he was on the grass, next to the limp body of Jeffries. The fire truck screamed around the corner. Bren would have to gather his wits if he was going to explain all this.

"What do you mean, Mel? Do you know about some cabin?" Hedy didn't understand as Mel pulled her inside.

"No, I don't know about any cabin but the county does." She began furiously tapping the screen of her phone.

"What, you mean like property records? The office probably isn't open but we could try calling."

"No, we don't need to. Pierce county has all their property records online and searchable. I can look for property owned by Jeffries within the county and if the cabin is in his name, we should find it." Hedy could hear the sirens right outside and she wondered if she should be out there, trying to help Bren and Darro.

"Jeffries, what's his first name, do you know?" Mel looked up from the screen and watched Hedy as she searched her memory.

"Ooh, it is...George, yes, George Jeffries." Hedy was normally terrible with names but she tried to make up rhymes to remember those she might need to recall. His rhyme had been the Jetsons' theme, as in Meet George Jeffries.

"Crap, here is the house on Griffin but nothing

else comes up under that name. Maybe it isn't in the county or it is someone else's cabin. Damn it, we'll never find her now!" Mel's voice was in a panic and she was practically wailing. Hedy was just about to tell her to calm down when another voice spoke.

"The grandfather, George Wilkenson" No riddles, no confusion from Adelaide. Just a simple name whispered in Hedy's ear.

"George Wilkenson. His grandfather's name." Mel looked at Hedy like she was crazy but she typed it in quickly.

"Here, here I found it! A parcel owned by George J. Wilkenson, up on Mount Enumclaw. It's about six miles from here. My phone's about to die, do you have paper so we can write down the address?" Hedy scrambled for a marker and she wrote down the address on a scrap of parchment paper.

"Let's go." Mel was up and heading toward the door before Hedy stopped her.

"No, you are staying here, with Bren. He needs help. I am going to the cabin."

"No way, you aren't going alone. You can't do this by yourself."

"Mel, listen. If you come, you could make things worse for Ana. You care about her and Lyssa might use that against her. I know you want to help, but stay here and help Bren. I'll bring her back. I promise."

"How are you going to do that?" Mel's voice

sounded desperate.

"With help, but a special kind." Hedy went into the entry and began checking the curio cabinet until she found a small knife.

"What is that? A knife?" Mel was not overly impressed by the small simple knife in Hedy's hand. What could she do with that?

"It's another relic from my family, older even than the shingle I showed you before. It's time to find out if the legend is true."

Hedy took the parchment paper with the address. Mel had just enough power in her phone to give her rough directions on where it was located before Hedy headed back outside.

"Help Darro with Bren. I'll bring her back." Hedy drove off leaving Mel at the curb.

CHAPTER TWENTY-FOUR

Hedy had a good sense of direction; given all the places she had lived in her life, it was a necessary skill she had picked up along the way. The directions had told her to head north, out of town toward Cumberland. Mount Enumclaw was near Lake Walker and though she had never been there before, she trusted she would be able to find it. She just hoped she wasn't too late.

There were only streaks of sunlight left in the sky, with long shadows and patches of darkness filing in the pastures as she drove. The meadows and grassy patches gave way to pockets of trees as she drove closer to her destination. Turning off passed the small state park on the country road leading to Lake Walker, the route began to curve and twist and the little bit of sunlight that remained was lost in the trees. She passed the Christmas tree farm and kept heading northwest, using the small compass on her dashboard and the flashlight in the front seat to navigate. Reaching the lake, she saw the towering form of Mount

Enumclaw behind it, blacker than the darkening sky. The shape of the mountain was like an anvil and she hoped that the cabin wasn't too far into those woods. Sense of direction or not, she could imagine getting easily lost on those old hunting trails.

The paved road ended and Hedy found the dirt road she needed, almost obscured by a huge thicket of blackberry bushes. She slowly followed the road, bumping along the potholes and ruts and she began to worry that the Corvair wouldn't be up to the challenge of this terrain. The road came to an abrupt end with a large metal barrier blocking the road and a weathered sign that read "private property". Hedy would have to continue on foot.

She grabbed the flashlight in one hand and the knife in the other and set off up the steep path leading into the darkness. The woods weren't terribly thick here, mostly scrub brush and young saplings; the area had been logged in recent years and the forest hadn't quite reclaimed it yet. As she walked through, the trees began to thicken and Hedy began to wonder if she would be able to find her way in the dark, even with her large flashlight. She climbed on, taking care not to trip over any tree roots or rocks as she went. A broken ankle could mean the end for Ana. The trail curved sharply and then Hedy found herself in a clearing, with a ramshackle cabin perched precariously against the hillside.

The cabin windows were boarded over but through the cracks, Hedy could see light. Someone was inside. She approached the cabin, walking carefully up the porch stairs, trying to step as lightly as she could. Wood that old would not be quiet and her steps sounded loud to her ears. Whoever was inside would surely know she was there.

The door to the cabin opened wide and the light from the oil lamps lit up the darkness. This was her invitation to come inside.

Hedy stepped into the cabin, clutching the knife tightly, feeling her heart now inside her throat. The room was small and the first thing that caught her attention was the smell. It had the overwhelming smell of a latrine.

"Well, if it isn't our intrepid baker, coming to pay us a call, ladies." Lyssa was standing near the only table in the room, which held the box stolen from the fruit cellar. Behind her, shackled together were Ana and two women.

"Ana, are you alright?" Hedy only glanced briefly at the Ana before stealing her eyes back on Lyssa.

"I'm alright, Hedy. We're alright." Ana's voice was steady as she spoke. The two women with her said nothing but they had been trapped in this cabin for much longer. Hedy had found the missing women.

"Oh yes, everyone is fine, Miss Leckermaul. In fact, you'll be able to take all three of them back to town with you, once I am finished." Lyssa spoke in a sing-song voice, as if they were somewhere much more pleasant than a stench-filled cabin in the darkening woods.

"What do you want? Leave them alone, please. You have the box, just go." Hedy stayed in front of the doorway, keeping an option of escape just in case Lyssa decided to step toward her.

"Oh yes, I have the box. It's funny, really. The box is something I have been looking for, for quite some time. When I finally found that peddler in Crete, he told me a strange American named Leckermaul had purchased it. You are what brought me to this little town. But now that I am here, I see this is the perfect place for me. So much rage, so much discord, so easy to provoke.

"Speaking of provoke, what little trinket have you brought with you, Miss Leckermaul. Is that a knife? How fitting for a baker, I suppose." Lyssa smiled as she lifted the wooden top off the box.

"Yes, it is a knife, a very old knife, a special knife, a knife that can harm even one such as you, Lyssa. Give me the women and we will leave this place and you will have your box. No one need be hurt." Hedy said and Lyssa laughed softly as she drew out the small terracotta vial from the box, sniffing at the opening.

"Hmm, imagine that, it still smells of marjoram." She threw the vial against the stone of the fireplace, where it shattered. The three women behind her shrieked, their chains rattling as they tried to pull away.

Hedy took a step forward, still clutching the

knife. She had never stabbed anyone, and until this day she would never have thought that she was capable, but it was all she had between her and harm for the women in the cabin.

"It is really amusing that you thought a knife could harm me. That I would be threatened by something so mundane. It would almost be charmingly naive, if I were incline to be charitable. But I am not." Lyssa picked up the small figurine and slowly unwound the linen around it. She brought the figure close to her face as she inspected it, turning it over carefully in her hands. "I always liked the Minotaur."

Lyssa smiled and smashed it against the stone. Hedy took another step forward, there was now only the table between them.

"I may not be like you, Lyssa, but you know my family history, surely. Did you think I would come here with some ordinary weapon?" Hedy raised the knife so that it shone in the oil lamp light.

"Oh, do tell. What makes your little pig-sticker so special, Miss Leckermaul?" Lyssa pulled out the arrowhead, the only thing in the box she was after.

"The world is full of stories, Lyssa. Especially the Black Forest, where my people are from. Enough stories for the Brothers Grimm to fill book after book. This little knife is not a fairy tale, it is real. It is an elfin blade, forever sharp, it can cut any flesh, even yours. It was given to my ancestor by the elf himself, a master bladesmith." Hedy watched as Lyssa turned the arrowtip over in her fingertips, tracing the jagged edge of one side.

"Oh indeed? How very impressive. Well, that is a special little blade then, but I don't think we will be needing it, Miss Leckermaul. As I said, you will be free to take your friends here with you. All I require of them is a small scratch. Surely that isn't worth much fuss." Lyssa turned slightly and smiled at Ana, who was closest to her.

"Why have you brought us here?" Ana spoke up, keeping herself between Lyssa and the two cowering women behind her.

"Well, this is far more dramatic than I really would have preferred but our Mr. Jeffries wanted to make an example of you three. You see, Mr. Jeffries, like his grandfather before him, cannot abide sin. And to his mind, you three women are just living, breathing sin. The woman teaching 'heathen ways' as he called it, the girl showing her naked flesh to sell coffee, and you, my dear undine, with your clear affection for that girl. Well, that was beyond bearing for Mr. Jeffries. All too easy for me to use. He wanted to purge your sins in fire and then dispose of you in these woods, as his grandfather had done in the past. Unfortunately for Mr. Jeffries, his usefulness was at an end and I need you all very much alive. You should be thanking me right now for saving you from his dark purposes."

Hedy started to move toward Lyssa but she was fully aware and she grabbed Ana's wrist, holding the arrowhead to a vein just under the skin.

"Oh, Miss Leckermaul, let's just stay still, shall

we? Don't make me harm these three beyond the small scratch I need. There is no reason for this to be more unpleasant than it already is."

"What is this scratch that you need? If you need to scratch someone, scratch me then." Hedy stayed still, trying to keep Lyssa talking until she could make a move with the knife.

"To be honest, you were going to be one of the three. I had planted the seed with Mr. Jeffries that you were a wanton woman, with strangers staying with you for who knows what purpose. But then our dear undine arrived, and changed my plans. For she is perfect for what I mean to do."

"And what is your plan, Lyssa?" Hedy had to stall for time. She needed an opening, something to help her save them all.

"My plan is the same as it has been since I was born, to bring rage to the world. To sow the seeds of discord and stoke the fires of madness. Nothing makes people easier to control than fear, fear for their families and fear of each other. This little arrow gives me the opportunity to bring havoc to this little town and watch it spread its tendrils to the city and the world beyond. All from a scratch, to three women. You didn't even know what you had when you bought this, did you, Miss. Leckermaul? Artemis' arrow kept in a cheap box with worthless trinkets."

Hedy had no idea what Lyssa was talking about. She knew nothing of any arrow of Artemis.

"You think this is genuine? This arrowhead?"

Hedy laughed hollowly, and for the first time, Lyssa seemed irritated. "You know the peddler I bought this from. Whatever makes you think this is anything but some old piece of Greek junk?"

"Well, let us find out, shall we? If it truly is an arrow of Artemis, a wound from it will bring disease to women and they will carry that disease with them, infecting others that they meet. A contagion spread from three unwilling hosts, and the best part is that every time our dear undine touches water, she will infect the water with it, carrying it further than I could have dreamed." Lyssa drew the jagged blade across Ana's wrist and a small streak of blood formed, bright against her skin.

"No!" Hedy tried to step forward but Lyssa grabbed Ana by the neck with her other hand, pressing the arrowhead against her jugular.

"As I said, let's not cause undue harm. I can kill our friend here and still see my plan through. The salamander was easy enough to dispatch, do you think I won't do the same to this girl?" Hedy felt helpless. If she tried to harm Lyssa, she'd likely cut Ana deeply or worse.

Ana began to laugh, a slow and ragged chuckle. Both Hedy and Lyssa looked at her.

"Is this the plan, then? To use me as your weapon?" Ana laughed louder, and the sound of it rang out through the cabin.

"This amuses you, undine?" Lyssa cocked her head slightly, bemused by the girl's laughter.

"Yes, it amuses me. Your plan is to use an unknown and untried weapon on me, hoping you can use my nature to amplify the danger. This certainly seems like madness to me, as is your nature. Madness rarely makes for the best plans."

"Well, we shall see, won't we? Perhaps you shall be right, but what if I am right after all?" Ana didn't have a chance to respond because there was a crashing thud against the side of the cabin.

In that moment, Hedy knew she wouldn't get another chance. Lyssa still had her hand on Ana's wrist but the noise had her startled and she had loosened her grip on Ana's neck. Hedy took the opportunity. In one move, she took the knife and stabbed deep into Lyssa's right side. The jagged blade sunk in to the hilt and Lyssa gave a curdling cry, releasing both hands in anguish.

There was a pounding thud as Darro barreled through the open door, hollering and howling as he came, making as much noise as possible, with Bren bringing up the rear.

"Darro, grab the arrowhead on the floor!" Hedy yelled. Lyssa crumbled before her on the ground, clutching at her side, flailing to grab the arrowhead before Darro could get it.

"Got it, Hedy." Darro clutched the arrowhead and put himself between the wailing Lyssa and Ana.

"Bren, get the girls out of here." The key to the shackles was on the table next to the box and he quickly opened the locks without the need to melt them. Shannon and Gretchen bawled with relief and ran blindly from the cabin. Ana stepped aside and stood next to Hedy, clutching the edge of her sleeve against the cut on her wrist.

"What should we do with this one?" Darro gave the figure of Lyssa a jerk of his head.

"A fire should solve things nicely." Bren looked darkly at the figure on the floor.

"No, we can't do that. We need her, to tell us how to cure Ana." Bren and Darro both looked quickly from Hedy to Ana.

"I know what to do, Hedy. The question is whether I will survive it. I need to get to contained water now."

"I'll take Ana to the house. You two should take the women to the police station. I think they are alright but there will be some explaining to do on how we found them."

"Don't worry. We'll tell the cops that the old git told us about the cabin and we figured it out. Still doesn't solve what we do about the hellion on the floor. Hey, wait!" Darro looked down and Lyssa was gone.

"Where did she go?" Bren hurried to the front door, looking into the dark. Only the two women were outside, holding on to each other, crying into the night.

"We'll worry about her later, for now we need to go." Hedy took Ana by the sleeve on her other wrist and led the girl out of the cabin. The men followed her out and they all followed the flashlight's beam out of the dark woods.

CHAPTER TWENTY-FIVE

Bren and Darro took the women in Darro's truck, heading toward the police station. For being locked up in the cabin for several days, they had few physical injuries, other than a state of shock at their rescue. It would be days later before they even began to wonder what all the talk about an undine and magic knives and arrows of Artemis even meant.

Ana and Hedy raced in the Corvair back to the house. Ana felt the poison in her blood; she had felt it the moment that Lyssa had cut her. She had no doubt that the danger Lyssa described was very real. If she didn't get it out of her system soon, she never would.

"What are you going to do, Ana? Do we need to call a doctor?" Even as Hedy said the words, she knew it was a crazy suggestion. What could a doctor do to help someone like Ana against some ancient poison on a mythological arrowhead?

"If I can get to water soon, I might still get it out of my body before it takes hold. We don't have much time though. Is Mel alright?" Ana felt the tears come to her eyes for the first time since that horrible man had grabbed her just in front of his house. She willed herself to stop.

"She's worried sick but she is fine. She will be so glad to see you." Hedy was pushing the limits of the car and trying to keep them on the road at the same time. She only hoped the police wouldn't be on the road back into town to see her speeding because she wasn't about to stop.

"I'm so glad she is alright. I wasn't sure if that man would hurt her. He grabbed me by his gate, putting some kind of rag over my face and when I woke up, I was shackled in that cabin with Gretchen and Shannon." Ana gulped hard and tried not to remember the horror of waking up in that place and the sickening smell.

"It's over now. Jeffries was badly burned in the fire started by Lyssa. I don't even know if he survived it. If Bren hadn't pulled him out, and Mel hadn't located the cabin, we would never have known where to find you." Ana felt the tears again try to flow and she squeezed her eyelids shut. She needed to keep the water in her body for now, every drop.

"Hedy, if I don't survive this, you need to get word to my mother. Her address is in my things. She must know that I haven't abandoned her."

"Stop talking like that. You are going to be alright. We haven't come this far to fail now, you hear me?" Hedy screeched the tires as she peeled onto Griffin Avenue and pulled up to the house. Jeffries' house was just a charred shell, with yellow caution tape strung all around it. She saw no fire truck at the curb.

Mel came bolting out of the house as soon as she saw the car, running across the lawn to grab Ana. "Mel, don't touch me, please!" Ana hated to yell at her but she couldn't take a risk of Mel touching her, not now.

"What? What's happened?" Mel looked stricken as Ana came across the lawn toward her.

"She's poisoned, Mel. You can't touch her right now, she has to get to water." Hedy led the way across the lawn, with Ana close on her heels and Mel keeping a short distance.

"We'll explain everything but we have to get Ana inside now." The three entered the house and Ana followed Hedy up the stairway toward Ana's room.

"Hedy, I need salt, sea salt if you have it. As much as you have. I'll need the bathtub full of salted water." Ana was feeling weak; the poison was moving through her body and she could feel it making its way toward her heart. It might be too late already.

"I'll get the salt. Mel, get the tub started." Hedy shouted at the girls as she ran toward the kitchen. She had a large carton of sea salt that she kept for her caramels. She hoped it would be enough.

"Mel, once the water is started, I need you to leave me. Whatever happens, please know that meeting you is the best thing that has ever happened to me." Ana wanted for all the world to give Mel a kiss and touch her face but she didn't dare risk spreading the poison.

"Ana, please let me stay in here with you." Hedy had joined them in the bathroom and was dumping the carton of salt into the water. Ana began to take off her clothes.

"Hedy, watch out for Mel, alright? Whatever happens, do not let this water drain out. It must not get into the sewer system. It will be contaminated with the poison. Get Bren to remove it. Tell him what I said and he'll know what to do."

Hedy led Mel from the bathroom as the girl was crying, trying to stay in the room with Ana.

"Mel, she needs quiet. Help her by waiting out here with me." The two sat on the edge of the bed, with the bathroom door between them and Ana. They didn't know how long they would need to sit there but they would wait. Neither had any idea what was happening on the other side of the door.

* * *

Bren and Darro were sitting in an interrogation room at the police station, with Shannon and Gretchen nowhere in sight. The women had come in, and were almost immediately whisked away to the hospital to be checked out. Bren and Darro were asked to wait in the room so an officer could take their statements. They hadn't had a moment alone to really discuss their stories but they each had come to the conclusion that the less they said the better. Apparently, they weren't suspects because the police had left them in the room together.

The Chief came into the room, carrying a notepad and taking a seat across the table from the two men.

"Well, we owe you both a big thank you, it sounds like. You found Gretchen and Shannon in the woods. How did you manage to do that?" The Chief gave them a blank look and clicked his pen. If he was thankful, he had a strange manner of showing it.

"The old man whose house burned down, Jeffries, he told Bren here while he was rescuing him. He said our friend was at his cabin in the woods." Darro had elected himself spokesperson for the pair.

"And why didn't you say anything to the officers or the firefighters on the scene of the fire?" The Chief was jotting down notes, keeping his eyes trained on Darro.

"Well, we weren't really sure if he was telling the truth. We never expected that the other women were there, we were only looking for our friend. He rambled on about her and mentioned the cabin, so we put two and two together, as it were, and thought we should check it out. She hadn't been gone long enough to contact the police." Darro was speaking quickly, hoping the story sounded plausible. The Chief said nothing for a moment but continued to write.

"And is this your story as well, Mr. uh...Aldebrand?" The Chief looked up at Bren who had been silent this whole time.

"Yes, sir. I am glad we were able to help those poor women. We got to the cabin and they were shackled up. Some crazy woman was there. She said she had been working with Jeffries. She got away though when we rescued the women." Chief Dixon continued to write, watching Bren closely.

"Yes, that is what we have heard from Shannon and Gretchen. They said that Jeffries kidnapped them, chained them up in the cabin, but this weird woman came tonight and was rambling about scratching them. They also said that Jeffries' neighbor was there, a Miss Leckermaul, and that she actually got there first."

"Yes, she was the first to figure out what Jeffries was saying. I was still recovering from the fire and wasn't able to leave until I had spoken with the firefighters. She made it to the cabin first."

"We will need to talk with her as well, this Miss Leckermaul. Why didn't she come to the station with you?"

"She took our friend back home, our friend just wanted to rest after her ordeal." Darro had piped up again.

"We'll need her statement as well. It can wait until the morning though. Jeffries isn't going anywhere; he's in bad shape at the hospital. We'll put an APB out for this woman, whoever she is." The Chief continued to write but he seemed to be finished with his questions for now.

"Don't leave town, OK? We'll need you to sign statements and I want you handy in case we have more questions. You can go home for tonight." Darro and Bren gratefully left the interrogation room and followed the Chief to the front door.

They both gave a large sigh of relief as they walked out into the night and headed quickly toward Darro's truck.

CHAPTER TWENTY-SIX

Hedy heard the front door open and she came out to the landing to see Bren and Darro come inside. She called back over her shoulder to Mel. "They are back." Mel didn't move from her perch on the bed.

"We're up here." Hedy came down the stairs toward Bren and Darrow, meeting them at the foot of the stairs.

"How's Ana?" The look on Hedy's face was all he needed to know.

"We don't know yet. We're waiting. How did it go for you?"

"The police will want your statement tomorrow, as well as Ana's, but so far they seem alright with our story. Jeffries' is in the hospital; they don't know if he will make it or not."

"Where do you think Lyssa went?" Bren looked from Hedy to Darro but both of them shook their head.

"I have no idea but maybe she's gone for good. That wound in her side would be a nasty one."

Hedy kept replaying the feeling of the knife penetrating Lyssa's flesh, like a raw pork roast, and she shuddered violently.

"What did she want? What was the plan with the box?" Hedy told them both what Lyssa had said about the arrowhead and the poison she was going to infect in the three women.

"So she used Jeffries and his obsession with sin to capture three women to infect?" Darro had missed out on much of the earlier conversations but he seemed to be catching up.

"Yes, she seemed to thrive on the chaos of it all. She said she used him and then she set the fire when she had no need of him anymore. She wanted the three of them alive, and he wanted them dead." Hedy shuddered again.

"And now what happens with Anahita?" Bren looked up toward the second floor.

"I don't know. She said though that whatever happens, that the water in the tub couldn't go down the drain. She said you would know how to get rid of it."

"How long do we wait?" Darro chimed in as Hedy turned and headed back up the stairs. She didn't want to leave Mel alone for too long.

"I don't know but I suspect if we don't hear something soon, we'll know the answer." Hedy led both men upstairs as they waited to hear from Ana.

* * *

Ana was sinking, down and down, below the water. The ancient lake of Urmia enveloped her, drawing her down to its center. She could taste the salt on her lips, and feel it surrounding every cell. Sinking below the depths, into the dark water, she felt the siren's call; how easy it would be to never rise, never rejoin the light but to stay there, in the dark, in the salty water and float amongst her ancestors.

"Child, you face a choice." The voice spoke to her within the water that was inside her ears, a voice that spoke softly in ancient Persian.

"You may stay and be one with water, for always, no harm or hurt or hunting, never harried by those that walk in the light." The voice was almost purring, the words dripping into her ears so softly.

"And if I return?" She said the words and they were carried away in a bubble of water.

"You may choose to return, it is not too late. But you will face longevity alone, without love, unless you dare love one who can prove true. But if you join us, your sisters, you will never be alone, you will never know pain." She heard other softer voices chanting "Join us, sister. Join us."

It was so seductive, the thought of just floating in this safe place, away from any fear or harm, surrounded by the ancient sisters who knew exactly what it meant to be undine. Anahita allowed herself to float calmly, taking in the brine of the lake and feeling the salt encasing her, forming a light crust on her skin.

But her mind began to think of Mel, and the days walking in the crisp fall sunshine, the soft kiss they had shared, the way her lips curled when she smiled, the feel of her hand. She would never know those days again if she stayed, if she let the salt encase her.

"Sister, stay with us. Let us keep you safe here, within the waters of your birthplace. Stay amongst your ancestors, we who know you." The voice was whispering again, drawing her deeper into the depths of the water. The pull was so strong. It would be all too easy to just let go.

Anahita knew her choice, she might fear the world with its pain, but she feared a world more where there was no love. The water was soothing but it lacked what she really craved.

"I will return." Almost immediately, the voice that had so lovingly caressed her now turned to a shriek in her mind. The salt grew harder on her skin, dragging her down, making it hard to move her body. It thickened and dried into an armor, making her heavy as a stone.

"Your place is here, with the undine." The voice hissed at her and she felt herself struggling to rise against the weight.

"You said I had a choice! You said I could return." She tried to thrash, to move her arms but they felt glued inside the cast of salt.

"Your choice is wrong, little undine. We will choose for you." The voice seemed to wrap itself around her and the weight of the salt seemed unbreakable.

With every ounce of strength she had, Ana began to force the water inside her body to flow out of her pores, pushing against the salt that encased her. The water, full of the Artemis poison could not be released; it was blocked by the force of the lake and her skin of salt. Anahita pushed as hard as she could muster.

She felt the cracking as the casing began to break and the water from inside her joined the water of the lake. She knew she wouldn't be able to rise and leave the water if she didn't push out the last drop of the watery poison from her body and so she continued to force it from her pores, squeezing out the very thing that kept her alive to rejoin the light.

"You will die, undine. You cannot live without water in your body, you who are a creature of water." The voice hissed again but this time with a note of fear.

"I will replenish, I will renew with the water of a new home, of a new place, with those who love me." Ana felt her body begin to rise, the last crumbs of salt releasing their grip on her skin and the weight leaving her limbs. She felt the grip of the water lessen and release her, even as she felt the last of the water leave her body, leaving her breathless and drowning in dryness.

Ana managed to break the surface of the water in the tub, forcing her arms up to the porcelain edge. She was so weak, she could barely hold herself from falling back into the water. She didn't think she could make it to the shower to restore the water she so desperately needed.

"Mel," she called weakly, afraid that her voice wouldn't be heard. But the sound carried just far enough and Mel hurried into the bathroom.

"Ana," Mel came toward her, appalled at how weak and drawn she looked, ashen gray and pale.

"The shower, help me." Ana tried to rise again but couldn't. Somehow Mel knew what she was trying to do. She came behind her and lifted her from under her arms. She felt almost light in her arms, with a kind of dried husk weightlessness. Mel helped Ana into the glass shower that stood next to the tub and she hurriedly turned on the faucet, flowing a flood of water over both Ana and herself. She held Ana up, keeping her facing the water and bracing her so she didn't fall. The water was cold but Mel didn't feel it. All she felt was the frail and weak frame of Ana leaning against her and that Mel had to be strong.

Moments passed and she felt Ana stir in her arms, starting to stand on her own feet strongly and lean less on Mel. Ana opened her mouth and let the water cascade down her throat. She blinked away the last traces of salt that clung to her eyelashes. She let the water pool around her feet and she felt her skin breathing in all the water and oxygen around her.

"Thank you, Mel." Ana's voice was still dry and strained but the color had come back to her face and she seemed to be stronger. She reached out and gently turned off the faucet, letting the last of the water drip down the drain.

"Are you alright now?" She loosened her grip around Ana and suddenly became aware that she was soaked to the skin in her clothes and Ana was completely naked. Mel kept her gaze looking up at the pale blue ceiling.

"Yes, I think I am. It was...difficult but the poison is out of my body, and now most of it is bound to the salt crystals." Ana took a step out of the shower, reaching for the large towel on the rack, wrapping it around herself before she turned back to face Mel. "I cannot thank you enough. I was not strong enough to make the final steps without you."

"I am glad I could help. And I am so glad you are alright." Mel stepped out of the shower, squelching in her Converse shoes and soaking the floor with the drip of her denim coat.

"We better get you something dry to wear. And I need Bren to help us get rid of the poisoned salt and the bathwater." Mel began to shed the wet coat, throwing it into the shower, as Hedy came into the bathroom, with Bren and Darro behind her.

"Everything alright?" Hedy looked at Mel

shivering in her wet clothes and then Ana, looking exhausted but alive.

"Yes, all is well now. Thanks to Mel. But we need to get her some dry clothes and we'll need Bren to help us clean up this mess."

"We can manage all that. Mel, come with me and let's get you changed. Ana, there is a robe hanging behind the door if you'd like. Come get Bren when you are ready." Hedy led the soaking wet girl from the bathroom and ushered the men out of the room into the hall.

CHAPTER TWENTY-SEVEN

Ana called to Bren once she had the robe wrapped around her and she had taken a moment to savor the fact that she was alive. Bren came back to the room and gripped the edge of the tub, warming the air and the metal of the cast iron tub just enough to cause the bathwater to evaporate. Ana would never have thought having a salamander in the house would come in so handy.

"I haven't thanked you yet. You saved me. Twice, really. You had every reason not to, after I accused you and pried into your life. So, thank you." Ana sat on the closed lid of the toilet as the last of the water evaporated into harmless steam, with most of the poison trapped in the remnants of salt at the bottom of the tub. He cupped the salt in his hands and melted the crystals into a puff of air.

"There is no need to thank me. I did what anyone would have done." He turned to face her and perched against the edge of the tub, the warm metal not bothering him.

"You saved Jeffries from the fire and he was the only one who could tell where we were taken. Anyone else would have left him to burn and saved themselves. And you came to the cabin and helped Hedy rescue me. If you hadn't come, things would have ended very differently. So please, let me just say thank you and to apologize again for doubting you. As you can imagine, trusting a salamander might not be my first instinct." Ana smiled softly.

"Alright, I accept your apology, Anahita of the undines. There, very formally and with respect, I have accepted both your apology and your thanks. Now, can we get out of here? I'm starving."

"Me too, strangely. And really thirsty."

"This calls for whiskey. Some good stuff, I bet Darro has some Glenlivet in that truck of his." Ana and Bren left the bathroom and headed downstairs to join the others, who were clearly cooking up something if the smells were to be believed.

"Oh, that smells like something wonderful, I am so hungry." Bren was the first to comment as they entered the kitchen. Mel and Darro were at the table and Hedy had a huge enameled cast-iron pot on the potbelly stove.

"Nothing fancy, but some lasagna soup and crusty bread. Vanquishing evil calls for cheese, pasta and soup. It will be ready in a few minutes, have a seat." Bren found a spot between Darro and a rather taciturn looking chinchilla, while Ana took the empty chair next to Mel. She had barely sat down before Mel wrapped an arm around her shoulders.

"Is anyone gonna explain why a rodent is at table?" Darro looked at the chinchilla and around the room at the smiling faces, all clearly in on the joke as far as he could tell.

"Oh, you've done it now, Darro. Maurice will never let us hear the end of it after being called a rodent." Hedy laughed and Darro looked at her with consternation.

"I dunna know what you mean by 'hear the end of it' but it's got eyes as black as the Earl of Hell's waistcoat and it is staring at me. I don't like it a bit." At this, Maurice gave him a disgusted stare and hopped from the table in a huff. The group broke out in laughter, all except poor Darro.

"We'll tell you later, old boy. Let's have a drink of whiskey and celebrate that we are all still here amongst the living." Bren took a bottle of Johnny Walker down from the shelf - it was no Glenlivet but it would do - and poured out a small glass for everyone, even the minor, Mel.

"Lang may yur lum reek!" Darro toasted the group and to that the group said cheers before tossing back the whiskey. Mel could be heard sputtering in the corner and though it tasted terrible, she liked the warmth as it spread down to her belly.

"Alright, before we get too carried away with this party, I need a few questions answered." Darro was already holding his glass aloft for Bren to refill, who obliged.

"How did you know where to find that old git's cabin? He didn't say anything to Bren when he came out of the fire."

Mel chimed in, placing her glass down on the table, upside down. "We tried to look up property records under his name but no cabin came up. If Hedy hadn't told me to look up the name 'Wilkerson', we never would have found it. How did you know his name?"

"Adelaide told me. I guess she is speaking to me again." Hedy said simply.

"Wilkerson, George Wilkerson, that was the name we found at the library, the one who was the suspect in the death in this house, back in the 1920s. Wilkerson must have been Jeffries' grandfather." Ana said, shivering, even in the warmth of the kitchen.

"Rotten fruit doesn't fall far from that old tree, does it? I haven't met whoever this Adelaide is, but I'd say we all owe her a dram of whiskey as well." Darro swallowed the second shot of whiskey, hoisting his glass in the air in salute to the unknown Adelaide. Again, the group broke out in laughter.

"I must be missing out on all the jokes around this place." Rising from his chair, he snatched an end off the loaf of bread on the counter before Hedy could stop him.

"Don't worry, Darro. We will fill you in on everything you have missed." Hedy poured in a mix of dried basil and oregano into the pot and room was full of the savory herbal scent that made everyone's stomach growl.

"I wasn't at the cabin, Hedy thought I should stay away, but how did you all get away from Lyssa? What happened to her?" Mel hadn't had the chance to ask anyone until then but she really wanted to know.

"Hedy managed to wound her, with that knife she brought. That thing seemed to have made a big wound for such a small blade. I'm guessing there is a story to that as well." Bren poured himself a bit more whiskey and offered the bottle to Ana, who surprisingly also took a bit more.

"That knife is actually mildly famous, for those who have read the Grimm fairy tales. It is mentioned in a tale called The Hand in the Rock. It's not a very famous story, and really not a very good one either, but the knife once belonged to an elf who would offer it to the girl he loved as she went every day to cut peat for her cruel stepmother. The blade could cut through anything. It's been in my family since before the days of the Grimms; supposedly my ancestor was the girl who received the blade, but who really knows. I took a chance that it would work on someone like Lyssa."

"An elfish knife? Fairy stories? You all are daft, no mistake. No wonder you have rodents at table for supper." Darro was shaking his head, clearly missing key elements to what had been happening over the last several days.

"So, you wounded her but what happened to

her? Did she run away?" Mel was worried that Lyssa might come back and try to harm Ana again.

"Honestly, I don't know. One minute she was there and the next she was gone, melting into the night. We never saw her go." Hedy stirred the soup clockwise, careful to avoid going the other way to avoid bad luck, because goodness knows they didn't need to push it.

"Well, let's hope that is the last we see of her. Maybe the wound was fatal." Bren gratefully took a bowl of the soup from Hedy, already planning his second helping. The worries of the forest and Greek demi-goddesses and arsonists were very far from the warm kitchen and the hot soup.

"I can think of someone I'd like to see the last of." Maurice chimed in from around the corner and Darro spilled nearly all his soup on his chest, howling as he did so.

* * *

After more soup, whiskey and several explanations about the nature of the house for Darro, everyone was ready to sleep. Mel had called her mother and let her know she was spending the night at her friend's house; she wasn't willing to go home just yet, not with the danger so recent. Darro too decided it was wiser to sleep on a sofa given the number of whiskeys he had consumed. He was serenading the house with a Scottish lullaby as he made his way to the sofa.

"Sweet the lavrock sings at morn,
Heraldin' in a bright new dawn.
Wee lambs, they coorie doon taegether
Alang with their ewies in the heather."

They heard Zelda hiss and Darro mumble apologies for no doubt stepping on her, before he started in on another refrain.

"The man sings like a bagpipe. Oof." Bren was relieved when Hedy closed the pocket door that lead from the kitchen to the shop, thereby effectively muffling the song. The girls had made their way upstairs, exhausted and grateful to be safe and together.

"You do provide your guests with excitement, Miss Leckermaul. I should be sure to let the Concierge know that for the next traveler." Bren was standing at her elbow by the sink, ready to dry the next dish that came out of the water with the warmth of his hands.

"Full service establishment here, sir. Bed, breakfast, kidnapping and arson. We aim to please." Hedy handed him the heavy pot and he had it dry in only a few moments. "Neat trick. Very handy."

He smiled and set the pot on the counter as she washed a platter.

"But seriously, I know Mel was thinking about it but what happens if Lyssa comes back." Hedy passed the platter to Bren and drained the water from the sink.

"I don't really know. I've already told the Concierge not to send any more travelers for now. I don't know if the risk is over or not. She might be dead, she might not, and I guess I'll just have to watch out for her until enough time has passed that I feel it is safe for visitors again. Not a very precise answer, I know."

"She looked like she was mortally wounded. That knife did a nasty cut to her side and even someone, something like Lyssa, likely couldn't withstand that."

"I don't know, I've never encountered a being like her. Sure, I've met plenty of travelers; nixies, sprites, a troll or two, a lycanthrope, and of course others of a more sinister nature, but never one that I truly felt would do me real harm, and harm to others." Hedy dried her hands on the edges of her apron and carefully hung it by the potbelly stove to dry. Alice was lightly whistling in her sleep from her perch.

"This was definitely a first for me. And, I'm not afraid to say, I hope a last time. Apparently small towns have too much excitement for me." Bren said and Hedy laughed, leading him out of the kitchen, when they heard Darro's snoring had replaced the singing.

"I'm not sure that snoring is an improvement over his singing." She settled in on the bottom step of the stairs. "Any news on whether Mr. Jeffries survived?" Hedy glanced over at the curio cabinet where the now-cleaned blade was resting back on its shelf; she imagined the questions she would have to answer for the police in the morning.

"We heard on the radio in Darro's truck as we were driving back that he was still in intensive care at the hospital. Burns like that will likely be fatal. The news is saying that he was behind the arsons and the man they had in custody has been released. They mentioned a woman of interest being at large but that is all they said about Lyssa."

At least there was some good news about the innocent man being freed. Hedy felt guilty that she had been so quick to believe the man was responsible.

"So, now that the mystery of the fires is over, will you be leaving for New York and your quest? I'm sure you are anxious to get on with your own journey."

"It's strange, up until today, nothing could have kept me from searching for the cure for what I am. I would have said being a salamander was the worst curse that could be laid on someone and I would give anything to be free of it. But in the course of a day, it was my ability to withstand fire, to save another from it, that ended up saving the lives of three innocent people. How do I walk away from that? Do I have an obligation to stay as I am?" Bren felt the pressure lift off his shoulders as he spoke. He had no answers but he realized just saying it out loud made the choice real and it helped to share it with Hedy.

"I can't advise you, Bren. I don't know what it is to walk in your shoes, to be what you are and see what you have seen. Only you will know what is the right thing for you, but I will say that I'm not sure I want to live in a world where people as wonderful as you and Ana don't exist. It's the whole reason I serve as a waystation host. This world is full of strange, complicated, unimaginable people and if we are lucky, we have the very good fortune to meet some and learn about them and spend some time with them. No matter what you choose to do, or why you are choosing to do it, you know that your very existence has meant life to some people. That alone is something to take with you always."

"I guess I have some thinking to do, assuming I will be able to sleep over Darro's snoring, but no matter what happens next, I want you to know that coming here and meeting you, Hedy Leckermaul, has been the strangest experience of my life. And for a salamander, that is saying something." Hedy gave him a playful shove in the arm before she stood up to head for bed. She had so much baking to do in the morning and it would be dawn before she knew it.

"Hedy, would you mind if I stayed on a few more days? I know you aren't officially a waystation right now but if you wouldn't mind putting up with a deliberating salamander, who is awfully handy at drying dishes, I could use the peace and quiet." He followed her up the stairs and she paused at the landing.

"Mr. Aldebrand, as it happens, I do happen to have room for you, and since you are such a hand with the dishes, perhaps you can lend me a hand in the shop tomorrow. I also have a tremendous amount of baking to do and you might be just the person to put in charge of baking bagels." He gave her a short bow before heading into his room and she continued on up to the third floor.

Maurice had found his corner and Zelda was curled up in the chair next to her door. The bedroom was dark and she was too tired to even turn on the lights. There was enough light coming in through the window to find her way as it was.

"She's safe." Adelaide ruffled the curtains near the bed and Hedy felt the breeze of her as she came by.

"Who, Ana? Yes, she is safe, thanks to you. The other two women are safe as well. We never would have found the cabin without your help, Adelaide. You saved them all. Thank you." Hedy unzipped her boots and stretched out her toes; it seemed years since that morning when she had put them on.

"Hate, envy, fear. It doesn't end." Adelaide whispered, close to Hedy's ear.

"I know, Adelaide. But that's the thing, the thing that you probably didn't get a chance to learn back when you were alive in this house. All those things don't end, and there will always be bad people doing bad things and bringing fear down on good people. But there will always be good people, people who bring hope, and love, and who stand up. Those things don't end either. And I believe they will win."

She waited to see if the spirit said anything more but she didn't and the curtain rustled again.

"You know what, Adelaide? It is late and I am rambling and maybe I will feel different in the morning. For now though, I'd like to think that love won out. At least for tonight. Tomorrow, who knows whether the danger will return but at least for tonight, we won."

Very softly, Adelaide whispered "Sleep well, I stand watch," leaving Hedy alone in her room. Hedy collapsed into the softness of her bed, too tired to even take off her clothes. She would deal with it all tomorrow.

* * *

Out in the night, in the dark remains of Jeffries' house, a darker shape watched the sleeping house. The slash in her side still throbbed, and she couldn't take her mortal form. For now, she could only exist as darkness, with yet darker eyes, pressing into the night, watching the house and waiting for her time to return. There would be time for revenge, time for the reckoning for what had happened. Lyssa was too weakened now, she would have to bid her time and find a dark place to rest and to heal. But she had all the time she needed and there would come a time when the meddling mortal would be alone and she would face Lyssa's wrath. All in due time. For now, Lyssa would gather her strength and call to her followers. The call of madness' mistress would be heard and they would converge to her beckoning. Her followers would make their way to this little town and bring destruction, piece by piece. She would see to the undine and her little friend, to the salamander and the oafish gardener, and of course, to the baker herself. The baker she would save for last.

In the shadows of Hedy's yard, Ren, the fox was awake and watching, keenly aware that something next door was not right. Something was there in the shadows and it was malevolent. Ren didn't know what it was or what it meant to do, but he knew it was there and he would be standing watch over the house tonight. He heard crows cawing, making far more noise than they should in the deep of the night, as if they were carrying a message along the wind. Other crows picked up the call and it carried as far away as his fox ears could pick up, which was quite far. He turned back toward the burned house and the darkness that had been there was gone. Only night time shadows filled the space, simple ashes and charred pieces of wood. Still, he would stay there in the garden until dawn and watch; it was what any respectable fox would do, especially one who owed a debt to the human inside. It would be light soon enough and he would pay a visit to the human and the creatures who dwelled there. He had to warn them.

Look for The Gingerbread Hag Book Two

IN THE TEETH OF IT

Coming soon!

Be sure to sign up for the newsletter at **www.kamiltimore.com** for more information on upcoming books and giveaways. You could win a chance to name a character in an upcoming book.

If you liked this book, please leave a review on Amazon and Goodreads and help spread the word.